IMAGINATION:
Passion Meeting Love

BETSEY GROBECKER

IMAGINATION: Passion Meeting Love

ISBN Number: 978-1-60571-613-8

Printed in the United States of America

Acknowledgment of Spiritual Mentors

Jyoti Chrystal: Shaman of Native American Tradition

Don Agustin Rivas Vasquez: Shaman and ayahuasquero
of Peruvian tradition

Yug Purush Swami Paramanand Ji Maharaj: Enlightened
saint and philosopher of Vedanta

Tobias and Adamus St. Germain:
Ascended masters whose essences are channeled through
Geoffrey Hoppe to bring forth teachings of New Energy
Consciousness

Mikael: Sovereign creator whose essence blends with
Robert Theiss to bring forth teachings of
New Energy Consciousness

Acknowledgment of Appreciated Authors

David Bohm: Theoretical physicist

Joseph Campbell: Mythologist and philosopher of religions

Fritjof Capra: Physicist and systems theorist

Carlos Castaneda: Anthropologist and mystic

Pamela Eakins: Sociologist and mystic

Meister Eckhart: Theologian, philosopher, and mystic

Matthew Fox: Priest theologian

Hans Furth: Developmental psychologist

Carl Jung: Psychologist and psychiatrist

Humberto Maturana: Biologist and philosopher

Jean Piaget: Biologist and genetic epistemologist

Ira Progoff: Depth psychologist and philosopher

Joseph Rael: Native American shaman and artist

Rupert Sheldrake: Biologist

Swami Chinmayananda: Hindu philosopher of Vedanta

Francisco Varela: Neuroscientist, biologist, and philosopher

PREFACE

This is a story about imagination. What I understand imagination to be is a radical departure from traditional thinking. I was once a researcher in Learning, Cognition, and Development, but what I had been taught about intelligence and creativity didn't resonate with me. Something was missing from within me, and from my work, that escaped my understanding. Unable to find answers in the science of my discipline, I left my university career to work with spiritual masters, worldwide. I also read the work of scientists who were breaking through existing assumptions of what defined life's essence. I was venturing upon the mythological journey to discover from within, what I could not find from without. What I share was gleaned from the wisdom touched within my inner depths, as well as authors and spiritual mentors, for you to experience as you wish. If the ideas challenge you, I encourage you not to give up. The story that follows will assist your understanding.

You may think imagination applies only to the Arts, but the imagination I speak of can never be limited to any one domain or action. It does not originate in the brain, nor can it be contained within the mind's dense space of reasoning and emotions. Its essence is so pure, so subtle and flowing, it cannot be entangled with any acts of "doing" by the mind and ego. Imagination is a sacred awareness, deep within the radiant void of your mind and body. It is your divine mind and heart: the creative passion of your spirit and the compassionate love of your soul.

Please do not confuse the figurehead of a judging God in Heaven, separate from you, with the divine heart and mind I speak of. This divinity is a Pure Awareness, a Consciousness, that is free of human attributes and of such passionate love that it wants only to share its radiance through you *as* You. You knew this divinity as a child when you lacked the power of logic. You also lacked an established sense of self, separate from your soul and spirit. Being of soul and spirit, your awareness was not contained within, nor was it defined by, your physical mind and body. Your actions were guided by your soul's intuitive, sacred breath that freely flowed within you. You *felt* the subtle essence of what you imagined, and from within that pure, malleable space of your existence, you took on the fundamental nature of what you imagined.

As your nervous system evolved in complexity, your awareness contracted into the density of this Earth realm. A center of self, separate from your soul and spirit, emerged in conjunction with the power of logical thought. Your ego mind is alive with charged thoughts and emotions that you have absorbed from others.

Deeply rooted within your biology, their energies act as the unrelenting judge to actions chosen. Every cause has an effect, and there is constant tension about which choice is best to act upon.

There is no one magical way to break this cycle of suffering, but there is always an intuitive nudge seeping through your awareness to seek completeness from within. After endless trials and errors, and steps forward and backward, your mind will slowly relax its tension to allow the loving breath of your soul to breathe through it, slowly dissolving hardened thoughts and emotions. Contracted space expands inward, until that magical moment when your purified breath touches your spirit's inspiration deep within the sacred, hollow chambers of your Beingness, then brings it forward into time.

You are most complete when the purified breath of your human mind and heart, *and* the breath of your divine mind and heart, breathe as a unified flow of passionate love. You assume an extended identity that is not only of your human mind and heart, but also of your soul and spirit. You are aware in the density of your adult, rational mind *and* the free-flowing space of your childhood, cosmic mind *and* the eternal mind of your spirit that transcends and illuminates all spacetime. You are the multidimensional Beingness of the holy magician. Your breath is the flow of love inward to touch your spirit's imagery within the hollow center of your Beingness, and outward to give this sacred inspiration material form. Realizing this state of Beingness, as a sovereign Self, is the greatest of all challenges on this beautiful planet we call Earth.

The characters in the story that follows reflect my own inner journey of finding a way out of the confusion inherent to leaving cherished beliefs and identities behind, repeatedly, to realize the wisdom within. There are also mentors, whose teachings reflect what I have come to understand. Each master, as the holy magi, guides each seeker through his or her unique magic. Breathe deeply while surrendering your breath to love and *feel* my words within a space freed of your mind's hardened beliefs and judgments. Read through the grace and great gift of your imagination and "Be" *as* imagination.

ONE

I was a music student, just beginning my senior year at a private college for the Arts in New York City. Music was my love and passion, and I gave little attention to anything else. I learned to play all woodwind instruments, but the flute, and its high-pitched companion the piccolo, were by far my favorite. They were the instruments I played in my college orchestra. I was the only male flutist in an orchestra with four flutists. I never understood the gender stereotypes related to instruments, and it was never an issue with my parents.

After I graduated high school, I called my parents Ethan and Iris instead of "dad" and "mom". It just happened one day after I left for college, and nobody objected. Being an adult myself, they were friends more than parents, and they treated me the same way.

Respect had always been shared between us. They never diminished or shamed me, even when the opportunity presented itself. They encouraged confidence in my abilities, and I trusted them in return.

Iris had majored in English with a minor in theater. Now, she was very active in the local theater group. She played the piano for the sheer joy it offered her at home. Ethan had majored in software engineering with a minor in music. He had played the violin throughout his schooling and now combined his love for music with his software skills. Famous musicians sought Ethan's esteemed talent as a musical engineer to enrich their music.

I had an apartment here in the city close to college, but I loved to go to the home I was raised in to relax. Tuning out the constant noise and activity of the city drained me, and I had to get away from it often. I was born into a wealthy family and grew up in an enchanting home on a large, wooded lot in Westchester County, New York. We all loved nature, and when the weather was good, we were bound to be outside. Today, I turned 21 and planned to go to my getaway tomorrow. Rain or shine, we celebrated my birthday on the deck that overlooked Iris' bountiful garden. Every year, Ethan gave Iris light blue irises for her garden, and Iris added red, orange, yellow, green, and violet to create a "rainbow" section in her garden. If she found navy or indigo, she added them. Iris said her garden was her second child she nurtured through her love. She suggested I enjoy the garden, too, as if it were my sibling.

I never questioned Iris and Ethan about why they did not have more kids. I figured it was their business, and if they felt it was important to share their choice with me, they would. The garden had become my friend, and I grew to appreciate it more each year. You may think this is a bit strange, but I could feel the garden's energy and the energy of the birds that played there. The smells and colors of the flowers, and the songs of the birds, enticed me into a deep space of relaxation. My worries and concerns left me. Sometimes, I saw the aura of plants perched above their tops. Next year, I wanted to plant a garden where I lived. I was currently looking at a few orchestras to play professionally for. My first choice was the Vermont Symphony Orchestra. I loved the country there and wanted to avoid large cities. My garden would be a place where magical memories were planted and lived on, just as memories were planted and lived on in Iris' garden.

Ever since I can remember, a crystal wine glass was placed at my seat overlooking the rainbow garden. What began as a couple of sips is now a crystal glass that accepted as much as it wished, although it was never refilled. Every sip was nectar that filled me and the atmosphere with its sweetness. It flavored my celebration with magical energy, and I needed to sip it slowly to feel every nuance of its nectar. Ethan and Iris never refilled their glasses either, but we all enjoyed what remained at dinner. That brand of wine and my crystal glass were used only on my birthday. They toasted with the same words every year. "To the very wise soul that sits before us. May we fill our bodies and minds with wisdom and love as we share our time together." Oddly enough, I never questioned what that toast was all about. Their words sang to my heart with such pure joy that I simply embraced the moment.

I was used to Iris' expressive voice and words, as she was immersed in theater work. She and Ethan encouraged my participation in the Arts, and I had attended private schools for the Arts throughout my schooling. After third grade, I left an hour early each day for my private flute lessons and the practice time I needed. The schools were designed to accommodate various artistic needs of students, and others also left early. Art was weaved within the curriculums, which were project-based. We were constantly challenged with questions that demanded critical thinking and evaluated our work with the teacher.

When I was a senior in high school, our class put on a Shakespeare play to show our understanding of psychological factors underlying human behavior. One student had difficulty owning the degree of aggressiveness his character held, and I shared his difficulty with Iris. "Acting is more difficult than it appears. The actor needs to delve into the unseen emotions and desires driving the character and own them as his or her own. Most likely, he doesn't want to feel his aggressive tendencies, as it may stain his self-image. I've learned a saint always has weaknesses, and a villain always has strengths. Our pretense of having only goodness shields us from acknowledging the dark shadows that hide deep within each of us."

"He seems to look for opportunities to help others and loves the accolades awarded for doing so. Yet, he almost begged to play this character."

"Acting aggressive tendencies of someone 'outside' of us is a safe way to express what we won't acknowledge 'within' us. I suppose we all project what we don't want to own, pointing the finger at others as the source of our poor behavior. Taught techniques do little if the actor lacks insight of the character's maturity intellectually, emotionally, and spiritually. Not so easy for anyone to achieve. Breaking habits of projecting blame externally, for what needs to be examined internally, is difficult even for adults.

"A wise soul once shared that grace has the power to transmute pain through its love if we allow it to. Our darkness needs acknowledgment, not displacement on others. I explore the depths of every character I act, wanting her to reveal how to be free of dark emotions that remain deeply burrowed within me. Even the goddesses I've acted, and who embody great powers, are filled with festering fear and anger. They play the same games of power and control humans play, seeking outside of themselves what they lack within. They suffer from their fears of what other gods and goddesses may do to them. Sometimes, it feels the drama among the gods and goddesses is even more intense than the drama we humans create."

Iris and Ethan could get quite deep at times. Yet, every time they went deep, their words impacted me in some meaningful way. That occasion was no exception. Afterward, I listened differently to the intense, low notes of my flute. They felt to express my gloom that I wanted to disown. I had always dreaded the darker notes in a musical piece and looked for distance from them. I started to feel deeply into my own cloud of sadness as I played these notes while listening to feel the sadness they wished to express. "Interesting how sadness is universally felt. Yet, each of us experiences it differently. My greatest sadness is related to my music," I thought one day.

In school, and during the years of my musical tutoring, there was much emphasis on learning technique and the secrets of various art pieces considered as classics. However, the secrets of what others believed created great Art did not resonate with me. I felt something was missing within me that beckoned its discovery. While my musical creations exemplified great technical mastery, they did not sing the deep beauty I desired them to sing. I often wondered if music created me, or if I was creating the music, then decided we created each other. So, the empty space looking to fill my music with great beauty also existed within me. "What creates inner beauty?" I often asked myself. "What needs to be uncovered to fill myself and my music with exquisite beauty?" I believed the revelation of what underlies masterful music would pierce through the dark cloud that hovered about me.

Ethan was a bit more "mainstream" in his words and actions, but his love and appreciation for Iris' sensitive and somewhat eccentric nature were evident. A raincloud hovered about Ethan, too, that threatened to rain on his future desires and visions should he let his guard down. Ethan existed in a void between the cultural norms of the business world and the art world. I learned in school that great artists practiced patience; they allowed their craft to unfold from their heart while nurturing and tweaking its emerging form over time. While Ethan was recognized for his creative works, he lacked patience. He was a master at perceiving the structural blueprint within music that few could match. He integrated the intricate patterns of music's elements to create unique accompaniments to the music of his clients. But as my high school years progressed, I sensed a repetition in his use of musical patterns and less experimentation with new possibilities. I didn't feel the enthusiastic inventiveness that once burned through him.

On those rare occasions when Ethan asked Iris for an opinion about his music, she said something like,

"Your music is brilliant, but I would like it to take me deeper into the feelings it could evoke in me." Iris spoke the truth, but her words fueled the dark cloud hovering about Ethan. He would nod, then withdraw into his sadness for a while. Like me, he just wanted this hovering sadness to disappear. So, he stayed away from any possibility of exploring how his computer-generated music could evoke the emotion Iris was looking for. Ethan once shared that his music was only meant to accompany the artist, and it was the responsibility of the artist to express emotional depth. Iris gave a slight nod as she walked outside to her garden.

Ethan always had ideas about how his computer-generated music could improve my music. All through school, I allowed whatever assistance he wanted to give me, which did improve my technical expertise. My music was highly regarded locally, and I had been frequently asked to play at events. Enjoying the opportunity to share my music, I seldom declined to do so. However, during my last two years of high school, a nagging sense that I needed space from Ethan's synthetic sound increased in its intensity. So, when I left for college, I told Ethan I did not want his musical input for a while. He accepted my choice, although I felt unspoken disappointment for refusing his help. Until that moment, I did not realize how much Ethan valued adding his sound to my music. I said that perhaps in the future, I would incorporate his music again, but I knew I never would. In my desire not to hurt him, I kept his false hope alive. I tried to convince myself that my "minor" deception was necessary, but deep down, I suffered from it. I just did not know a peaceful way out of this conflict other than to pretend I would fulfill his hope in the future.

My music defined me. It was my first, and currently, only love. I protected it as one protects a lover. I dated before, and shared beautiful moments with girls I had been with, but I had no interest in participating in activities expected in a relationship. Idle chatter with others about things that had little importance to me drained my energy. It was not fair, to me or others, to pretend to be interested in things I had no interest in. I suppose others would consider me as a loner. Occasionally, I would go places with someone from school, but I usually declined to do so. I wanted the best for everyone, and gave help when needed, but I did not want to feel responsible for their emotional well-being. I felt somewhat selfish for not being as involved in the lives of others as they wished me to. But I had learned from experience that it was easier to live with what I considered to be a flaw, than to have to deal with the consequences of not following my nudges and getting involved.

It seemed that every relationship had entanglements centered around emotions. The drama in Shakespeare's plays lived in all of us to some degree, and I was disliking human drama more and more. I believed that is why I enjoyed Ethan and Iris so much. The space we shared never felt heavy or burdened with emotions. Occasionally, disagreements arose, but free of cynical feelings, they never lingered. They did not want me dependent on them, and I did not want them dependent on me. I came and went as I pleased, but respected them, and their space, when we shared time together.

As I matured into my adolescence, they told me I must live with the consequences of my own actions. They would share advice, but the choices made were mine to own. Even when I sought advice, they responded with more questions than answers. Now managing my life as a college student, I appreciated how they guided me through my life's challenges. I saw escalating drama in the lives of my peers as they blamed family and friends for their problems; it was a dog always chasing after its own tail. This fruitless action just kept repeating the same action and reaction.

TWO

I t was evening on a refreshingly cool, Friday night in early September, and I was doing my usual walk in Greenwich Village to find just the right music café. I always wished to discover a talented new artist, but tonight I also wanted to use my license to buy my first legal glass of wine. I passed a café I had visited before and felt a nudge to turn around. Sometimes, I would get a sense that I should do something, and I usually trusted those nudges. So, I turned around. On the window was the schedule of the artists and the content of their performances. It was breaktime now, but in a very short time a woman I had never heard of, Micaela, would be performing a ballad about the angels of faith, hope, and love. "No Preaching," it said. I visited this café often and never had a bad experience. "Be adventurous," I told myself, "after all, I can now enjoy a glass of wine while listening to music."

The place was surprisingly packed, but as I entered someone got up to leave. "Perfect timing," I thought. "I suppose I was meant to hear this woman." When I ordered my wine and showed my now legal ID, I was given a glass "on the house" to celebrate my formal entry into the adult world, and those at my table gave a cheerful birthday toast. As we chatted, Micaela walked on stage. None of them had heard of Micaela either, but like me, they felt a nudge to listen to her. The sounds of the violin as she warmed it up began to pierce through our conversation, and we stopped talking to listen. The lighthearted chatter filling the place when I entered succumbed to a beckoning silence of unusual stillness. All attention was fully on Micaela. "That's odd," I thought. "I've never seen people stop their chatter to listen to a warmup."

Micaela was a rather small woman in height and weight, but her size was deceptive to her presence. Her physical features suggested her age to be about 10 years older than Ethan and Iris, although her body dimmed to a shadow in the immense peace she radiated. Every string she touched sang a serenity that gently massaged my body while relaxing me. Never had music touched me with such depth. I breathed deeply as I closed my eyes. "Is it possible Micaela will reveal what I've been searching for?" I asked myself. I surrendered to the vibration of the notes, asking them to reveal any magic they held. She ended her warmup, let the silence deepen into our space for a few moments, then began to play her violin as I have never heard a violin sing before.

My mind and body relaxed deeply, softening tensions I did not realize I was holding. With my eyes now closed, and my entire body soothed by the gentle caress of her magical notes, my vision surrendered itself to its energy. I felt like I was drifting into a dream state, but I continued to hear Micaela's violin. Surrendering into my semi-wakeful state, Micaela's violin became a canoe adrift in dark, salty waters of what I sensed to be a womb. The space resonated with a sacredness I had never known. Its cleansing, saltwater breeze whispered notes of serenity, easing any fear of its pitch-black waters. The water received the soft breeze that hugged its surface, rippling slightly, while rocking my canoe upon its buoyant waters. As notes floated into the higher octaves, vibrating strings of light appeared on the water's surface, then infused themselves within its sacred darkness. Their intense heat created clouds of salty mists that enveloped me in their compassionate droplets. The tempo of Micaela's music quickened, and my canoe rocked playfully with the water's dancing vibrations of light and dark.

Slowly, gradually, the joyful violin notes were transformed into sharp, aggressive notes. Boastful of their expert technique, the notes devoured the air's joy-filled whispers, and the water's compassionate mists. A bright, red flame appeared in the water ahead. The notes became more forceful as their wild, assertive energy fanned the flame's intensity with their self-righteous roar. The expanding flame sucked in the air surrounding it to feed its vigor, creating a vortex whirlpool in the water that pulled my canoe toward it. Now surrounding the entire outer edge of the vortex, the flame seemed unconcerned that it could engulf my canoe with me in it. I desperately wanted to escape, but I had no paddle. My panicked fear fed the flame while smothering the space between me, and it, with its uncompromising force.

A sense of hopelessness to escape the flame's resolute passion filled my cells with rekindled tension. I recalled Iris' words to have faith that I am always protected when I feel fear. But my hopelessness would not allow any comfort faith could offer. Micaela began to magically intermingle what had been separate musical octaves and tempos. The compassionate mists returned, caressing the intense flame and my tense body with their loving droplets. The flame's stark colors dissipated into a soft, golden glow that blanketed its calm upon the water. The force of my body's panic, now soothed by the compassionate mists, loosened its demanding grip on me. The immense love that now filled the flame teased me to release the remaining tension of my panicked fear. Slowly, my body began to yield its fear to this sacredness, but its hardened shell blocked the fullness of the flame's sacred presence.

A pure, white flame with a gray luster at its center arose from within the still center of the vortex. For a few moments, it rested in its place as it radiated a sensuous passion. I sensed it welcoming me to join its mysterious, sacred space, but only after I stopped empowering fear and doubt. It descended, taking any remaining turbulence in the air and water with it. My canoe rocked gently again back and forth, up, and down, just like the rhythm of my calming breath. The more deeply I surrendered to the flow of the water's pulsating rhythm, the more my fear yielded to its calming presence.

The violin music ended. After a few moments of silence Micaela introduced her ballad as "The Enslavement of Hope, Faith, and Love" and began to sing. I opened my eyes a bit, wanting to watch her sing every word. Her voice, filled with the radiance of the flame's purified light, weaved its presence through the silence. My eyes, clouded by its beauty, closed to better receive every nuance of its sound.

> The angel of faith believed in God's holy will.
> For unanswered prayers, she kept her doubt still.
> Her deep trust, the heavenly God would salute.
> Her devotion, the heavenly God would reward.
> Her faith, surrendered to an external God,
>   she fulfilled.
>
> Ceaseless mind control kept her doubt and mistrust
>   at bay.
> The fullness of the moment, lost to a future say.
> Exhaustion, incompleteness, restlessness, gnawing
>   fear:
> Is this the price of faith the angel must now pay?
>
> The angel of hope trusted liberation was near.
> No matter how bad, he did not yield to despair.

His expectation, the heavenly God would salute.
His future, the heavenly God would reward.
His hope, surrendered to an external God, was his
    fare.

Ceaseless mind control kept his fear and despair at
    bay.
The fullness of the moment, lost to a future say.
Exhaustion, incompleteness, restlessness, gnawing
    fear:
Is this the price of hope the angel must now pay?

The angel of love practiced charity without dismay.
For the neighbors and the poor, he altered his say.
His compassion, the heavenly God would salute.
His generosity, the heavenly God would reward.
His love, surrendered to an external God, was his
    way.

Ceaseless mind control kept his motives and needs
    at bay.
The fullness of the moment, lost to a future say.
Exhaustion, incompleteness, restlessness, gnawing
    fear:
Is this the price of love the angel must now pay?

We are the angels of hope, faith, and love . . .
And claiming our inner divinity frees us from
    despair, fear, and pain.
Faith, the yield to the inner movement of wisdom's
    flow, will we embrace?
Hope, the promise of spirit's imagery carried forth
    into time, will we breathe?
Divine love, the nectar that resolves entanglement
    with opposites, will we sense?

Will spirit's passion, bathed in intuitive waters of
    love, be our guiding flame?

Silence entered the room as her voice slowly left its
space. I felt like I was coming out of a deep sleep, except
I had heard every word she sang. Slowly, gradually,
people began to clap. Perhaps they, too, were coming
out of a trance-like state the music had induced in them.
I opened my eyes, looking for my hands to acknowledge
the artistic magic of her music. While I could not put
my finger on exactly what her music offered, I knew it
was what I had been searching for. A calm, easy chatter
slowly began to fill the room. Looking at the serenity in
the faces and eyes of the people at my table, I knew they,
too, had a deeply moving experience.

Micaela had already left the stage when a chorus for
an encore arose. The host came on stage saying she must
hold to the schedule and move on. I looked at the time and
realized Micaela had been playing for over a half hour.
It seemed like less than five minutes. Becoming more
present in my body, I felt an exhaustion I seldom felt. I
needed to leave but wanted to initiate a small conversation
with Micaela first. Just as I stood to look for her, Micaela
was standing at my side holding a folded piece of paper.

"It's rare to have the honor of sharing the birthday
celebration with a full-fledged adult. I'd like to buy you
a drink to celebrate sometime soon. If you're interested,
send a note to my email."

I must have taken the paper because I found it in my hand when I left. All I could remember was pushing my chair in, then finding her already gone when I turned around. No one at my table even seemed to notice Micaela standing by me, or my leaving. The cool night air to walk in provided grounding to my body that was still floating on the buoyant waters. I wondered if something was in the wine that created my sensations and visions. If it were not for that piece of paper in my hands, with Micaela's email and words to her song, I would have passed the whole night off as a mind-trip. Yet, at some level, I sensed what I experienced was very real. It was the same feeling I knew when I woke up from a dream that I sensed to be real, but that my logical mind wanted to negate as possible. I also recalled vague memories of this lightness as a kid. Thankfully, sleep engulfed me as soon as my head found its welcoming pillow.

I awoke to a cool breeze from my bedroom window. It was Saturday, and I needed to get a few things done before catching a train to Westchester. But I laid in bed for a short time longer, enjoying the freshness the breeze offered. Closing my eyes, I breathed in synchrony with its gentle, caressing rhythm. It playfully wrapped itself around me, teasing me with the suggestion of taking flight. My lighthearted spirit took me back in time to when I was a kid enjoying magical play with the plants and animals in Iris' garden. I remembered seeing the light of nature devas within the plants. Others, in the schools I had attended, were sensitive to feeling and seeing nature's light, too. We learned that science did not acknowledge nature as aware with its own consciousness, but we were encouraged to feel into our own truth and question what did not feel right. We had to provide evidence for our beliefs, even if it was "unscientific" data sourced from the "sight" of our intuitive imagination. I still had a painting I made of lights in trees as evidence for the existence of nature devas.

I smiled at the thought of seeing Iris and Ethan, as well as the cook, Antonio. He had been with us since I was a kid in preschool. Like my family, he also had artistic "quirks". We all learned to say Antonio's name as he wished us to: as a song that carried joy and love. More than once, a gnawing sadness was dissolved just by saying his name. When I said it in a manner that especially pleased him, Antonio's huge, black eyes, glimmering with a light that made his somewhat chubby, tall body almost disappear, acknowledged his pleasure. I could not help but to return his joy. Antonio worked only a few hours each week. Ethan and Iris both enjoyed cooking, but they needed extra help, mainly on weekends, due to their frequent entertaining related to their work. I was glad he worked a few hours most weekends. When he took the weekend off, I missed him. But his joyful presence so permeated the space of the house, that whether his body was present or not, I felt Antonio's joy as a constant occupant.

Iris' creative nature never accepted routines, and she challenged Antonio with one new recipe each month. She was a bit of a health fanatic and always looking for ways to enhance the variety and flavor of healthy foods. If a recipe did not work out, Antonio reminded us that his primary ingredient was love, and his love was never compromised. He never depreciated himself or his creations. Antonio was raised in an Italian family, and his mother taught him how to cook at his request. I believed she also taught him how to say his name. It had to have been a loving relationship, just as my relationship with Iris was loving.

When I finally sat up and saw the paper Micaela gave me on my bedside table, last night returned to me. I took it into my hands to check if Micaela's song and email were still on it. Everything was there in black and white. I could not deny the events of last night. I started to read the ballad's words before I stepped into the shower, but my attention was unfocused, and I gave up. When the shower water began to flow, flickers of the white flame from last night appeared within it. "I know that flame from somewhere," I thought but was too light-headed to place the memory. I opened the cold-water valve to feel planted on this Earth and not floating in the sky. I wondered if Micaela felt like she was floating when she played. Was this feeling of lightness related to the magic of her music?

My passion to discover what was missing from within me, and my music, gave me the courage not to be completely unhinged by my experience and negate it. Deep within, there was a familiarity with the beauty I experienced that gave credence to it. I had to understand why Micaela's music touched me as it did, regardless of the doubts and discomforts I felt to do so. Like Antonio's passion for cooking, my musical passion was not something I would compromise. I planned to look at the ballad's words on the train, but instead, I soaked in the majestic beauty of the compassion I continued to experience. I did not want it to stop as it soothed every part of my being. "Better than any massage I've ever had," I thought. I felt a deep love for Iris at some point, appreciating her in a new light. She had a way with men that loosened their masculine edges that society deemed necessary. I even saw that with Ethan's father, Darren.

Darren was a stockbroker, specializing in hedge funds, and a multimillionaire. Our house was a "small" wedding gift to their son and daughter-in-law as Ethan's parents referred to it. Darren's seriousness and intellectual intensity could cut through a rock, but Iris would not interact with him by entertaining his intellect. She would have him walking through her garden, smelling the roses so to speak. His intense, serious demeanor always softened when around Iris. Florence, his wife, appreciated Iris' gentle touch with Darren. Most times, she would wait on the deck, or in the sunroom, enjoying special coffees and desserts Antonio had made for her. I did not know if she enjoyed Antonio or his creations more because I heard her laugh often around him. To cut through Florence's "uptight" demeanor was not an easy feat. The stresses Darren and Florence entered with, mellowed significantly by the time they left. But by their next visit, any relaxation they had softened to had left them. I wondered if they were even aware of how much tension they held. It seemed they accepted their stress as a natural way of being, never questioning its presence.

THREE

"Happy Birthday, Dakari!" Antonio said as his glimmering eyes greeted me at the house. "I trust the world is gifting you an exquisite day today. Would you like a cappuccino?"

I usually checked my mood before saying his name, but my joy-filled "hello" flowed from me without any prep time necessary. Antonio's entire being responded with pure pleasure as his smile, and the gleam in his black eyes, widened.

"I'd love to have one but hold off for now. I need some time to get settled. Where is everyone?"

"Ethan is meeting with a musician. He'll be back in a couple of hours. Iris is out doing some errands. She's been gone for a while and will be back shortly."

He returned to the kitchen. I went to my bedroom and freshened up. My bed looked inviting, and I laid down to relax while allowing the compassion that continued to radiate its presence to enter ever deeper within me. About a half hour later, I called down to Antonio to start making my drink. I had not yet discovered a cappuccino that matched the deliciousness of Antonio's, even in Little Italy. He knew I was always ready for one when I arrived.

When I started to go into the kitchen to claim my coffee, Antonio stopped me. "Sorry, but the chef is at work and can't be distracted. Iris is back. She's outside on the deck waiting for you." He handed me my tantalizing drink, and I left him to his craft.

"Dakari, my love, Happy Birthday!" I never tired of Iris' greeting, regardless of her specific words. She held a warmth few people matched. Her blue eyes and shoulder-length, strawberry-blonde hair glowed, especially when we sat on the deck on a sunny day. Her love for theater lived through her being, just as my music lived through my being. Now and then, some theater people would visit. They also spoke with greater expression than most. But some seemed to be "performing" an act, as the tone in their words expressed pompousness. Perhaps, they were hiding their truth from themselves as well.

While lost in my musing, Iris gave me a small, loving hug that I barely acknowledged. She commented on how peaceful I seemed. "Did you do something special for your birthday?"

"I heard a woman named Micaela sing and play her violin last night at a music café. Her violin and voice enchanted me." I was silent for a couple of minutes, searching for a way to describe Micaela's music, and my experience with it. Pensively, I shared most of what I had experienced as I tried to make sense of it. "Never before has music affected me like this. Part of me wants to discover what was in her music that moved me so intensely, but another part of me warns of caution with the unknown. Is her music safe to explore? Was what I felt just a trick of my mind that made what was unreal, appear real?"

Iris shook her head slightly, acknowledging my words, then slowly sipped her tea as she looked out at her garden. After some time, she returned her attention to me. "Ever since the earth was churned to create my garden, and the seeds and plants slowly added, it became a well of beauty and love for me to drink from. When I tend to my outer garden, I'm also tending to my inner garden. It's the dark soil within, filled with seeds that want to birth their deepest glory. Perhaps my own caution of the unknown and untested, that my fear creates, is my greatest deterrent to breaking through into the darkest layers of my inner soil where nothing from the outside can affect its peace. I believe this pure space, deep within me, is where my sacred beauty lies.

"I recently told you that at your birth, I touched a space of profound, compassionate love, and I've spent the past 21 years trying to breathe its life back into me. At that time, I held off on the details of my experience, but I sense it's time to share them with you. When I was in the early part of my labor, I refused painkillers, as I wanted to be fully clear at your birth. When my pain became unbearable, and I asked for pain relief it was too late to change my decision. As you were moving into the birth canal, I panicked from fatigue and pain. I'd been in labor for two days and complications were emerging. Your heart rate increased to a level that could harm you. My own physical body was going into distress.

"My doctor, a woman I respected, assured me all was well and not to panic. She said to put my full concentration on relaxing through my breath as I had practiced. While breathing, an intense, luminous light began to fill space around me. Opening to its compassionate depths, I felt lifted into a sacred realm of intense majesty. Freed of the heaviness of my fear, my awareness left my body. I saw my body on the bed, surrounded by harsh lights and irritating sounds of various instruments. I also felt the doctor's hidden anxiety to save us. I didn't want to return to the harsh world where my body was in distress. When my eyes fell on Ethan, he appeared lost in the bliss I knew. Believing he could manage without me, I was ready to leave the world, in great peace, to save you.

"A stunning, oval egg of luminous light slowly descended toward my physical body, which I knew to be your soul. You radiated an unspeakable, sacred love that communicated to my heart with a clarity I had never known and have never re-experienced. The loving sensations of your message etched themselves within my heart, never to be forgotten. When these sensations felt complete, I knew I had to reenter my body to birth your human form and raise you. As I reentered, I embraced, in love, the dark unknown of my womb that I had been fearing. Your birth was quick and without further pain and complication. About an hour after you were born, I asked for paper and pen to write what I said was a private reflection of your birth, and your soul's words flowed onto the paper. My doctor later shared she had never witnessed such a dramatic change in vital signs so quickly. I told her I had found a deep place of acceptance for all that was, as it was, and released my fear. Come into the garden, and I will share your soul's message."

Iris put her arm out to embrace mine as we silently walked to her garden. The last remains of the dew on the ground from the cool night glistened in the sunshine of the early fall. We sat on the bench surrounded by iris flowers. At one end of the bench, close to where Iris sat, a silver angel rested on a black, granite pedestal, placed there soon after my birth. The lightweight angel was held in place at its base by silver hooks attached to its heavy pedestal. Iris took the angel into the house to bathe and polish it frequently, along with its crown.

I had always been attracted to this angel. It did not have a name because Iris believed its form felt too transparent to be identified with a sex or trait that would contain its presence. It was two feet tall with wings fully extending outward from its arched back, just below its neck. A graceful strength radiated from its wings that shined even without the sun's presence. The iris of each eye was unpainted, but the area enclosing each silver iris was painted pure white, and the pupils painted black. I often sensed a glowing light within its black pupils that invited me into them. When I did not resist the calling to peer into its eyes, I felt great serenity. However, I had yet to find the courage to enter the depths its eyes teased me with, and my fear always closed the opened entry.

The palms of the angel's hands were open as if to draw the sun's light into them. Iris placed fresh flowers into them daily, even in the deepest cold of winter. Often, Iris tied flowers to a vine that flowed from the angel's hands, over its body. A small, delicate crown of golden twigs sat on her head, always adorned with fresh baby breath and daisies that protected the gold from the elements. When harsh weather passed through, Iris took its crown into the house. On each foot was an ivory lotus. The angel's silver, metallic gown appeared to transmute its substance into silk at times to flow with the winds that whispered vibrations of peace. I never questioned what I saw, just as I never questioned the words to my birthday toast. The angel was sacred. Its presence blended with the plants and animals in a garden whose magical essence remained undeniable.

Elegantly sketched in the black granite of its pedestal was an intricate design of two serpents that overlapped each other at various points, while forming three, enclosed circles. These circles increased in circumference as they ascended to the pedestal's top. A white flame, with a small, gray oval at its center, was painted within the black granite of the middle circle. I realized it was a close duplicate of the flame I saw last night. "Amazing, no wonder the flame in my vision felt familiar." I also recalled this flame in a carving Antonio had gifted me on my seventeenth birthday.

While lost in my musing of the angel, Iris had unfastened the silver hooks at the angel's base, then carefully lifted the angel into her lap. Sliding its base open, she retrieved a piece of silk paper with writing on it. I did not know its base opened, or that it was hollow inside. "No wonder it's so light," I thought.

"This is what my heart received from your soul. Read it through the compassion you're now feeling. It must be heard through your heart's love to receive what it wishes to share. I've learned through the years to relax my mind and feel the essence the words carry. They always touch me differently. Take all the time you need."

I took the paper into my hands, breathed the compassion I continued to feel deep within, and silently began to read it:

We are on Earth to remember that we are so much more than our mind and body. We are soul and spirit, too. Spirit is the brilliant blaze of Pure Consciousness whose creative potentials lie deep within the sacred void of our body's empty cavities. Through a fiery passion to create in its own image, spirit's potentials are thrust outward into the compassionate, nonfluid waters of our intuitive mind: the divine mind of our soul. Within this radiant darkness of our innermost chambers, spirit's imagery is nurtured and prepared, until ready to be brought forward into linear time through the breath.

But this vast, dynamic space of creation's imagery is veiled by the forceful, dense chatter of our hardened thoughts and emotions. Their impurities fill space with fear and judgment, suffocating the breath's expansion into its subtle, sacred depths. Unable to touch and carry spirit's creativity forward into time, the breath deadens to inspiration. We free the breath of its shallow, stagnant flow by ending our entanglement with fear and judgment. Inner battles between opposites are surrendered to fill our minds and bodies with ever more radiant love. Every battle surrendered in love relaxes the tense breath of our rational mind, helping to dissolve the force that separates it from the free-flowing breath of our intuitive mind. The inner world of spirit's imagery, and the outer world of human form, slowly come into balance.

When the human *and* spirit breathe through a unified, sacred breath of love, our being is vibrantly alive in divine passion. This sacred breath flows inward to our intuitive depths, and outward into linear time to birth creations of profound beauty. The artist and the artwork have completed and expanded the other. But all that is born, will decay, returning to the void to be restructured and born as renewed life. Life's wisdom forever expands inward to the infinite love of Self and outward to heighten the vibrancy of experience.

Allow my imagination to soar as a child. It is the divinity of my soul and spirit expressed through me *as* Me. Do not fear the light in my eyes. This light is my spirit perceiving through them. Play with me as a child, and you will rediscover the joy of your own spirit's play. In my adolescence, my soul and spirit will be less present as my mind takes on the density of space and time. I must uncover the light within the depths of the radiant darkness to realize a love free of fear.

I had no idea how long I stared at the words. At some point, I realized I was breathing deeply as if wanting to touch the sensations the words spoke. They felt vaguely familiar, just as my experience of last night felt vaguely familiar. But like last night, I could not fully take them in because they challenged who I knew myself to be. When I handed the paper back, Iris told me to keep it. She returned the angel to its pedestal, handing the ownership of its message to me. Right now, I wasn't quite sure who accepted the paper. How I knew myself had just been shattered into fragments. I recalled brief conversations with Antonio, right here in the garden, speaking of my soul as my intuitive Self. His words always pierced me in a magical way that I had grown used to when being with Antonio. But as I grew, this magic felt to remain in the garden, seemingly removed from influencing my life.

We were silent. If ever there was a time to feel the garden's sacred magic, that time was now. "Breathe in the garden's peaceful presence," I kept saying to myself. "Do not panic." Ever so slowly, as I breathed the garden's calm within, I found space from the tightening grip of my panic.

Iris began to speak softly. "Ethan and I have been waiting to share these words with you. You had to be ready to own the responsibility they engender. We've been feeling the time has come, and your experience last night erased any doubt. I believe Micaela called you into the café to initiate you into life's hidden mysteries. Ethan will be relieved that it's finally time to share his experience with you. We've done our best, but we're also on our own inner journeys. We can't provide you with the assistance you now need.

"We wanted to keep the love we had awakened to during your birth alive, but it has dimmed greatly with the passing of time, just as the intensity of the love you experienced last night is beginning to dim. We studied

Eastern philosophy and experimented with different meditation techniques, adapting beliefs and techniques in ways that felt comfortable to each of us. My garden is my space of meditation, and Ethan's space is his music studio. During the winter, the sunroom is my meditation space as I nurture myself with its many plants. But I spend time in my garden each day, even on the coldest days, while placing fresh flowers on the angel.

"Over the years, the life cycle of my garden has deepened its presence within me while also teaching me. The wisdom each season offers is the wisdom I embrace. Now, my garden is surrendering its living tissue to decay, offering its decomposing matter to the soil microbes that provide nutrients and fertilizers for new life. I'm more aware of what's living within me that needs to be offered to the Earth. But I can release only what my mind will recognize as decay. Its fears of change, the death to life energies that must leave, are not easily overcome. It seems the more I attempt to lessen resistance to release decayed life, the more forceful its resistance becomes.

"Earth's bareness during winter encourages my inner stillness. But my stillness is not true peace. I know my inner chatter is merely subdued by pushing it further inside, adding to my mind's cluttered space. I want to merge with the vigorous roar of my spirit's winter breath to clear the space of my hardened thoughts and emotions to know clarity, but the flow of cleansing breath through me is blocked by the hardened wall of my charged thoughts. While soaking my iris seeds in mid-February, I imagine the compassionate love of Earth's waters churning energies that wish to remain embedded in my cells, transmuting them into soft iris petals that yield to the slightest whisper of summer's breath."

Iris stopped speaking while staring at the angel. She appeared lost in deep contemplation with it, and I did not disturb her. At some point she continued, although her gaze remained on the angel as if speaking to it. It was no secret that Iris talked to the angel. I did, too, although I never admitted that fact to anyone.

"I break Earth's silence in early March. Loosening its frozen surface to plant seeds, I envision the fortifications of my mind's resistance relaxing. Throughout the spring, as the warming sun and Earth's waters nurture the seedlings, I also absorb the nurturance of the sun and water. When my garden radiates its full splendor in the fiery heat of summer, I radiate new life that has bloomed within me no matter how minimal it may feel. But the ever-present hum of fear's taunting dims my radiance as it forcefully asserts its belief that what I experienced at your birth was a daydream to escape my pain. 'Nothing within requires change,' fear tells me.

"Faith that I will again experience the sacred light I knew at your birth keeps me going. I have dreams where this angel embraces me with its light-filled wings. The serpents of its black base come to life as well as my fear of them. The angel guides me to look into the blackness of the serpents' eyes to see their compassionate glow. 'Darkness is present to teach us how to embrace fear, for it is within the darkest fear that we find the light of the most exalted love. Feel your fear completely and release it to Earth in love. The serpent embodies the compassionate wisdom of Earth's waters and will lovingly ingest whatever you offer it. It does not recognize fear as real.' But I cringe at what its dark eyes may reveal and look away."

Iris sighed. Birds chattered loudly as they flew from a tree, circling around us with their play. We shared a welcomed laugh that eased the intense energy of her words. I had been listening intently to Iris, trying to absorb the integrity her words held, and her profound passion to rediscover the love she experienced 21 years ago. So much had happened so quickly, and it overwhelmed me. I told her I needed time alone. Iris smiled, then walked to the house.

FOUR

After Iris left, my space of solitude filled with noisy chatter. Endless questions, doubts, and fears surfaced as overbearing monsters that demanded attention. And yet, I could not deny the beauty of last night, which Iris just confirmed. It had to be real. The air held a fruity sweetness as the irises released their life breath to decay. They were hybrid seeds that bloomed in spring, summer, and early fall. Breathing their sweetness into my depths, my body received their nectar as if to receive an extravagant dessert. Inner chatter calmed itself. "Just breathe," I told myself. "Don't think."

Relaxing more, a sleepiness came over me, and I surrendered to it. In my dream, I saw Iris standing in her summer garden among irises that had peaked into the full glory of their colors. I was present as well but off to the side where she could not see me. The vibrancy of the colors far exceeded anything I had ever witnessed. Peering deeply into their mesmerizing hues, I heard their vibrations sing the sound of woodwind instruments. There were seven distinct pitches that ranged from low to high. Listening intently to the purity of their tone, I watched in awe as the irises magically transformed into instruments. The red irises played the lowest-pitched tone of a saxophone, orange a bassoon, yellow a clarinet, green an English horn, blue an oboe, indigo a flute, and the violet irises played the highest-pitched tone of a piccolo. While there were distinct tones of each instrument, I also heard a unified sound of joyful celebration, enticing me to join their magical creation.

While joyfully playing my flute, my back arched into a humpback that held rainbow-colored iris seeds. I scattered the seeds about as my flute magically played through its own powers. The red, low tones of the saxophone pulled me inward to a darkness whose love softened the intensity of my creative passion. The high, intense tones of the piccolo propelled my nurtured passion forward into time to be shared. All was in perfect harmony, unified in deep joy, as the seeds of life's renewed beauty were sowed.

A wind blew in, blowing its breath through the instruments, transforming them into their original form as matured irises. I again stood off to the side where Iris could not see me. Sensing her immense joy, I believed she had witnessed what I did. The wind strengthened its force, freeing the irises of their roots. Spiraling clockwise, they clustered together with their matching color, from lowest to highest vibration, on both sides of Iris. As the irises yielded their form to the sacred vibration of their color, an arc began to form around her. Pure love weaved itself throughout the burgeoning rainbow-colored arc as if to bind the distinct vibrations each color sang.

Just before the sides of the arc were to join above Iris' head, the Earth below her opened, creating a vacuum of air. The white flame of last night emerged from within the Earth's opened void. I recognized its compassion as the love that felt to bind the colors. The flame rested above the opened hole, unaffected by the turbulent winds around it. The rainbow, surrendering to the suction of the void, swirled above the flame in a counterclockwise spiral. Shortly before its vibrant colors merged with the flame, they collapsed together as a unified vibration of blazing, white light. The still sacredness of the white flame continued to radiate its majesty, undisturbed.

Iris, however, was far from silent. She did not see the flame, nor did she feel its loving majesty because she was panicking in fear for her safety. Her eyes filled with fear's darkness, and her body stiffened with fear's tension. She was calling out to God while pleading for His mercy to keep her safe. Her resistance created chaos about her. I wanted to tell her she was safe; there was danger only if she resisted. But I could not speak. Slowly,

I became aware of Ethan's voice. Realizing he was not in my dream, I tried to wake myself up.

"Dakari, are you awake? Looks like you were sleeping. I hope I didn't startle you. Happy Birthday! I just returned home and came to the garden thinking you and Iris would be here enjoying this beautiful day. At least I found you. Antonio said brunch would be ready in 10 minutes. Does that sound good to you?"

Ethan's brown eyes that I inherited, reflected his pleasure seeing me. I gratefully received the warmth of his greeting. Ethan was not much taller than Iris who was average height and weight for a woman. His slight frame and somewhat small height for a man was hidden by his intense presence. Iris' colorful warmth never overpowered Ethan. Instead, it glowed on him as a soft light that balanced the strength of his intensity. My height and small frame mirrored Ethan's, but I lacked his poise. There were times when I felt energy from others, much taller and muscular than myself, attempting to intimidate me with what they perceived as an "advantage" over me. At those times, I imagined the warm glow of the garden shutting out the impact of their energy. I walked on, not engaging in the exchange of energy they desired, even if not spoken verbally.

"Hi. Yeah, I was having an intense dream. Ten minutes sounds good. I'll join you on the deck then." Ten minutes was not much time, and I needed to splash water on my face to orient myself.

"I'll look for Iris and check in with her about time. I'll let you know if it's going to change," Ethan said as he began to walk away.

My birthday brunch was on the deck inviting celebration. Ethan filled my crystal glass and their glasses with my special wine. When the toast was given, it felt to announce a profound, new beginning. Sipping my wine slowly, while engaging each sense fully in the experience, I reached deep into its essence to unveil the secrets of its sweet nectar. The wine became my blood, containing within its essence the secrets of my soul. My splintering identity made me feel light-headed. I tried to eat the enticing Italian food before me, but I barely touched it.

Iris observed my absent presence and asked Ethan about his morning. He talked about a young, new artist who was gaining popularity quickly. He was concerned the artist was taking on too much, too fast. "She doesn't understand that fame can take over her life. Her innocence is a moving presence in her music, but promoters are taking advantage of her naivety. It's not my place to coach her, but I shared a story about a musician I knew who withdrew from the world for a while to find a balance between his fans and his music."

Ethan's vision was almost always filled with hope. I often felt his hovering sadness was due to feelings of doubt about the quality of his computer-generated music he did not want to acknowledge, but he sensed. I now understood why Ethan felt that way. He had a mystical experience at my birth and would never be the same. Everything was shifting. Having just witnessed the harm panic can do, I told myself that support is present. I just needed to find space from my fear to feel this support.

Iris kept Ethan occupied in a conversation about this artist and others as brunch continued. When we celebrated with my cake, I told Ethan a little about Micaela and what Iris shared. I said I wanted to hear how he experienced my birth, but not until dinner. I needed some time alone.

"I'm relieved Iris shared the words of your soul. I can understand your need for space now. No wonder you were so quiet. I thought you weren't feeling well and didn't want us to know. I'm glad you're not getting sick. I'd love to share my experience with you at dinner. I've waited years to do so."

I left them and went to my room. I read and reread the words of my very own soul until I could no longer take them in. I recalled the carvings Antonio had gifted me over the years. Every birthday, since I turned four, he gave me a carving of an animal or mythical figure. He said he imagined the words the figure wanted to tell me and wrote them on a small card. Before I started college, we would sit on the bench next to the angel as I opened my gift and read the card. The words never ceased to dance off their surface and into my heart.

This time together was most special when I was young, and it was raining. Antonio's big, black umbrella was a magical tent that raindrops fell from as a stream of light. "Why do raindrops turn into a stream of light after they fall on your umbrella?" I had asked.

"Because the glimmer in my dark eyes likes to dance with the raindrops. If you want the glimmer in your eyes to dance with them, just see your light within the dark droplets. Light is always present to lift you into magical realms, but you must believe it exists, even in the deepest darkness. Imagine the magical light in the dark and open to receive and radiate its joyful dance."

"That dance of magical light is exactly what I had witnessed as Micaela played, and as a young kid, I knew the joy of that dance," I realized in wonder. But as the years passed, the words challenged my mind. Somehow, the presence of Antonio and the angel gave credence to the words in a way I could not fully understand. I felt lifted from my mind as if to exist beyond its logic. I was that innocent child again, open to the magical wonders of the world.

On my seventeenth birthday, my last birthday before leaving for college, Antonio told me it was the last time he would be with me as I opened his gift. "It's time to feel the energy the carvings carry without my guidance. Their energies want to live through you, but you must receive them in your heart to know them. The angel is here to still your mind should you need help to do so. The allowance of your soul's love, through your breath, will help to unveil your divine heart and mind deep within the empty cavities of your Beingness."

He handed me the colorfully wrapped box that contained my gift. I was astonished when I saw the carving because it looked like me. Above my navel was a black oval with the white flame of the angel's pedestal at its center.

"Antonio, you said you carve only sacred figures, but I believe this figure is me."

"Read the card, Dakari. Let it guide you to answer your own questions. There's no one correct answer. There's only the answer that makes sense to you in the moment as you evolve in divine love. As your understanding is transformed, your questions and answers will change. Even if your words are unchanged, the resonance of the wisdom they carry will deepen. Then one day, there are no more questions because you have realized the sacred Mystery residing within the deepest darkness of your body's sacred chambers. Never feel foolish to sit with the angel. I promise you it will guide you wisely if you allow its love-filled wisdom to do so. Relax your mind while expanding your breath inward through love. Wisdom is an intuitive sense, not black and white statements to be analyzed."

I nodded, sensing the deep wisdom of his words. I read the card aloud, "Feel the fiery passion of your spirit weaving its potentials within the dark, creative matrix of your soul. Empty your breath of its tensions and expand it inward to touch spirit's imagery. Breathe its inspiration into your flute. Create music of true passion."

I sighed, wondering how the pure magic I had shared with him dimmed. Antonio once told us he enjoyed mythology and carving figures of various spiritual traditions. Even Ethan and Iris had a few of his carvings. I knew they valued them because other than a vase that always held fresh flowers, and a small tiffany lamp whose top held the rainbow colors, they were the only items on the marble table that occupied a large space under the sunroom's bay window. Light always glistened on the carvings, even on the cloudiest days, casting an image of the lamp's rainbow colors on them.

I recalled a recent conversation with Iris and Ethan. They had shared how difficult change was when the energy of fear continued to plague them.

"Growing up in my Irish Catholic family, I learned I was born with sin and tempted to sin. This belief created much shame and guilt for my imperfections," Iris said through a voice soaked in sadness. "To lack faith in God to grant eternal salvation from sin, removed any chance of God's forgiveness for my evil tendencies. I was doomed to eternity in Hell. So, my mind's fear of God's punishment, not my heart's love, guided my behavior.

"After a mystical experience during your birth, I could no longer accept these words. I was enveloped in a love so sacred that judgment could not exist within it. I questioned what darkness really is. My womb, that nurtured and birthed the seeds of light to create you, and my garden's soil, that nurtures and births the seeds of light to create my garden, are of the dark. A balance within the light and the dark was missing. The sacred love I lost myself to at your birth was without judgment. And if God is this love, then His judgment cannot exist. My faith is no longer based on a need to receive God's absolution for my faults. My faith is that I will be assisted in releasing the shame and guilt that seem to prevent me from feeling the love I knew at your birth."

Iris' earnest words left me unsettled. I was glad when Ethan began to talk. It eased my growing discomfort.

"I also had an experience with sacred light when you were born, although it was different. It deepened my creativity in extraordinary ways. Like Iris, I stopped believing in a judging God after you were born. But even though I meditate each day to release my self-judgment, it remains. The creativity I felt at your birth was extraordinary; it didn't feel to be of this human realm. I meditate with the hope that I will one day know this transcendent creativity again."

They had never spoken about my birth before or of any mystical experience. After being silent for some time debating whether I wanted to hear more, my curiosity exceeded my resistance. "Will you share your experiences now?"

They looked into each other's eyes for a couple of minutes while nodding a slight no. "What will be shared with you is profound, and we must wait a little longer for you to be prepared to hear as you need to. We'll know when the time is right, and I sense it'll be very soon," Ethan said through a promising voice.

"Wise decision on their part," I thought. I was not ready to hear what was just shared, even two months ago. The compassionate love now making its presence known made it possible to feel the truth of my soul's words. But even with this compassion, the words confused my mind and provoked fear. I understood they trusted the words of my soul only because their heart had been opened to the pure vibrations the words held. I rolled the silk paper, enclosing it with the silver ribbon that had wrapped my gift given to me at lunch. It was my first flute made of a gold and silver blend. I wanted this flute for a long time. Delicately lifting it from its case, I touched each key, and its keyhole, while closing my eyes and envisioning the sound I wanted to create through it. "Sacred sound," I thought. Recalling the tune of Micaela's ballad, I began to recreate it. I put my full focus on my breath, wanting to feel its sacred life force pierce through me, just as I felt the sacredness within Micaela's music pierce through me.

Placing my flute below my mouth, my breath flowed into its open mouth to be given form as notes. When playing the low notes, I lost myself to the sensations of the dark, salty water and the lustrous light diffused within its essence. Reaching into the higher octaves, I felt the fiery passion of my own breath creating the notes through my instrument. I understood that if not soothed and nurtured by the water that contained its life force, my fiery passion would burn out-of-control. The turbulent winds of my semi-dream state as Micaela played were the turbulence of my own breath that felt panicked. It was a breath fed by my fears of what was ahead. Just as Iris feared the unknown when the Earth opened, I also experienced this fear. Would I trust and step into the center of my shattered sense of self to experience the bliss within the white flame? Right now, I did not know.

FIVE

If no company came on weekends, dinner was kept simple. Before his early departure, Antonio prepared a casserole with leftovers that were warming in the oven. I never appreciated that simplicity as much as I did now. The wine and my crystal glass remained on the table. Before sitting down, I filled my glass more than usual to help relax my disjointed mind. Iris told Ethan not to concern himself with getting food on the table. He could sit and enjoy the wine as she gathered dinner. I usually helped as well, but it did not even cross my mind to do so. I wanted to be still as if the stillness of my body could bring about a stillness to my inner turbulence. Ethan also poured a substantial amount of wine into his glass after he sat. After a few slow sips, he began to talk.

"This afternoon, I was in my studio hoping to re-experience the intense, vibrant light I felt at your birth.

I seek the return of that light daily as I meditate while listening to music. It was a light that lifted my entire beingness into a state of deep peace and joy. Prior to feeling this peace, I was fearing the worst of what could happen to both of you. I broke into a panicked sweat when I believed Iris was giving up and would die. When the doctor assured her that all was well, reminding her to breathe as practiced, I started to breathe with her to help both of us move through our increasing panic. With every breath, I became more relaxed. Encouraged by the relief my breathing offered, I allowed each breath to expand deeper within me. For a while, Iris and I were breathing in a synchronized rhythm, supporting each other through our breath. At some point I closed my eyes, losing myself to a bliss that overcame me. Every sense was enveloped in an unexplainable sensation of sacredness, and I yielded to the support I sensed from it.

"The instruments monitoring the vital signs of both of you became intensely harsh, and I thought I may have to leave the room. But then I became aware of soft, meditative music in the background. Giving my entire focus to its sounds, I lost my awareness of everything else around me. The notes danced with an intricacy between each musical element that I didn't know was possible. They were stripped of all unnecessary complexity and heaviness to unveil their most subtle beauty. These keen, pure notes, flowing within a compassionate nectar, weaved themselves within my breath filling every cell with their essence. I knew only profound beauty."

I saw tears come to Ethan's eyes for the first time ever, and he did not try to hide them. He stopped talking to breathe deeply, closing his eyes for a couple of minutes before continuing.

"When I heard a flute in the music, a figure emerged who resembled the mythical Native American humpback and flutist, Kokopelli. The joy his magical flute emitted as he played vibrated with sacred purity. I knew Native Americans believed Kokopelli possessed the seeds of wisdom and fertility within his humped back. He planted his seeds throughout the spring while blowing his sacred breath through his flute. A bounty of crops always grew for those left behind. I believed this figure was you, seeding much needed joy and love into this world. So, I was not surprised when you told Iris and me that you wanted to play the flute when you were only five years old. We had various instruments for you to play, but we were careful not to influence your preference of instrument. It was for you to decide, not us."

Ethan again stopped and sipped wine. His intense focus was lost to a space within him, as if touching the space of my birth, and his voice sang the vibrations of love he was lost to. I, too, felt lost within a space of pure, vibrating love. Anything was possible, even seeing my back "humped" as I played magical notes in the garden, and Ethan "coincidentally" sharing his sacred experience with Kokopelli. Antonio was wise not to tell me Kokopelli's name when he handed me the carving of him on my sixth birthday. My accumulated life-experiences enabled me to recognize a wisdom in Kokopelli that my childhood eyes could not have grasped.

"I have no idea how long I was in that experience," Ethan voiced after some time. "Your cry took me out of what I now believe was a sacred space my awareness had entered into. I looked at Iris who was glowing in the radiant joy I felt. I knew she also had a profound experience. When you were handed to us, we wept with joy and relief. Your presence was of profound love, and we were unified within that love."

Ethan's eyes again filled with tears as he became quiet. I noticed Iris sitting with us, her eyes filled with tears that the table was absorbing. "You've witnessed all without judgment," I silently acknowledged to the table while moving my appreciative hand over its surface.

"Neither of us could speak of our experience for some time, but we recognized change in us. Iris was quieter and stiller than usual. She went to a few garden nurseries to buy an angel statue for the garden. When nothing appealed to her, we looked for a craftsman to make what Iris envisioned with the same result. A couple of months later, we were celebrating our anniversary in a rural area of the Catskill Mountains. Passing a home with an exquisitely carved angel overlooking the garden, we pulled over to inquire about it. The woman who answered the door said a craftsman, who does not meet with people personally, made the angel. She would give our phone number to him but warned that most times he doesn't call people back. If he wanted to call us, we would hear from him within a week.

"Two days after we got home, Iris received a call from a private, unlisted number. It was the craftsman. Iris spoke to him for quite some time, describing her experience at your birth. She said she felt his acknowledgment of every word she spoke as if he fully understood the depths of what she had experienced. When she was done speaking, he described his vision of the angel and its pedestal, and Iris was thrilled. She didn't want to change anything. He provided a post office address to send a deposit, and six months later, it was delivered. Iris paid more than what he asked, saying its worth was beyond any monetary value.

"When the angel was placed in the garden, Iris held a silk paper. She said it had the words your soul spoke to her at your birth, and she wanted to share them with me. As I read the words silently, Iris voiced each word that was etched within her heart. I read and reread them before Iris placed the paper inside the angel's silver body. It was a bright, sunny day, and the angel's face appeared to light up as the words were placed within it. I sensed it welcoming your soul's words, inviting me to do the same. While I didn't understand most of them, their profound truth touched a knowingness deep within me. It was early spring, and the birds were just starting to return to the garden, blessing it with their songs.

"Perhaps because we could no longer contain our

experiences, they flowed from us with the angel as our witness. Since then, Iris has kept fresh flowers in the angel's open hands. That following winter, I began the tradition of giving Iris blue iris seeds for her garden, and Iris began the tradition of finding other seeds to complete the colors of the rainbow. Blue irises symbolize hope and faith, and I sensed they belonged at the lotus feet of the angel."

Ethan stopped again, sipping his wine. Iris' body was still, her eyes vacant, as were Ethan's eyes.

"Like Iris, I became quieter, and my mind more still. But unlike Iris, my body was active as I created from this sacred space of inner calm. I experimented with creating the perfection of sound that had filled my being, readily sensing, and removing unnecessary complexity. I blended different musical elements in ways I was unable to do before and fed those patterns into my computer to create new patterns. But I was unable to replicate the sacred resonance of the sound through my computer programming, and it was that resonance that gave the notes their magical quality.

"When you were young, I often went into the garden to sit by the angel while reading the message of your soul. I felt a deeper sense of connection to the words there. It was difficult not to analyze each word, which just got in the way of hearing your message. I laughed at an intuitive sense that the angel's energy was helping to create an open space to receive the wisdom your soul's words held.

I finally came to accept that your soul's wisdom could only be known from a space deep within me that was not of my mind's logic. But I also knew the intense clarity of that space was lessening with each passing day.

"One day, while Iris was tenderly washing the angel, I told her about my experiences with it. Iris said she believed the angel guided her from within a space she couldn't rationalize but felt. She didn't want to intellectually dissect what she sensed because her words couldn't depict the majesty of the angel's presence. But I persisted with my hope, my belief, that it was only a matter of time before I would mechanically replicate the sacred sound I sought. When I played my violin, I came closer to recreating that resonance, but my computer-generated music could not even begin to approach the sacredness I had experienced.

"However, even with this limitation, there came a time when I was ready to share my new sound, and my music spread like wildfire. Famous musicians wanted my sound, offering more than others to secure my work. Slowly, insidiously, I ignored my knowing that my music didn't hold the deepest beauty I wanted to create, losing myself to the growing accolades from musicians. My play with you when you were young, particularly when we were in the garden, kept reminding me of life's sacred resonance I was attempting to ignore. When you reached your early teen years, and we no longer shared that play, I could completely ignore my inner knowing that what I had experienced was lost to a formula to follow for success. I stopped trying to create that sound, even on my violin.

"When you left for college and said you wanted to take a break from my musical input, I knew you sensed what I had been trying to deny. But even then, I couldn't consciously affirm those limitations to myself. This afternoon, I finally accepted that I got lost in the status and wealth my music provided while forfeiting my initial passion to recreate the sacred sound I was gifted with experiencing. I've suffered from my choices, and it's time to begin to release what no longer serves my music and my creativity."

The breeze had picked up as he talked, bringing the sweet smell of the maturing irises. "Perhaps," I thought, "Ethan's own beliefs about himself, and the music he created, had ripened beyond their full maturity, and it was time to face his forceful resistance to change."

My own self-deception of hope for good outcomes with Ethan's music also came forward to be recognized. I was not ready to share my dream in the garden, but I could acknowledge my own untruths to Ethan. I sighed deeply. "I wasn't being honest with you when I said that in the future, I'd use your music again. You validated my gut feeling that something is missing from your synthetic music and from my own music. Micaela's violin sang with the sacredness you once knew. I believe she can help me discover what I need to find. She heard the people at the table toast my twenty-first birthday, and before she left, she offered to buy me a drink to celebrate. She gave me her email if I wanted to accept her offer. I was undecided about contacting her, but I'm now sure I need to do so. On that same paper are the words to her ballad. It's as if she knew I'd be there and wrote those words specifically for me, maybe for all of us. I'd like to share the words with both of you, but let's wait until tomorrow. Right now, I need to take a long walk."

They said they would love to see the words as they began to clear the dishes. I started to help, but they said it was my birthday, and I was free. I didn't argue with their offer. I needed space, lots of space.

Fall was my favorite season. In no other part of the country did I witness the variety and richness of leaf colors than here in the northeast. As a kid, I had great fun raking leaves into large piles and jumping into them. Such simple things brought such great joy. Until all the leaves left the trees, I insisted my place at the table have a placemat I loved making by pressing leaves between wax paper. Admiring their colors as I once did as a kid, they glimmered in the sunshine. I breathed deeply, wishing to open my senses to hear the vibration their colors sang.

I recalled my first day as a college freshman when my orchestra conductor was going through introductions with new students. He was moving down the roster of names while asking students ahead of me questions related to their past experiences and passions with music. His small, but robust middle-aged body assumed the stature of a giant as he perched upon his high, conductor podium. He was welcoming, yet intimidating, at the same time. Clearly, his standards were high, and I was concerned I could meet the challenges ahead. I heard little of what people before me said because I was pondering what to share.

"Dakari," I heard him say in his resounding voice, "what are your passions with your music?"

I froze, completely unprepared to answer. My passion, however, did not freeze, and it was my passion that spoke as my voice. "Music gives my life purpose and fulfillment. I'd be lost without it. I want to create a sound that holds deep passion, but something is missing from myself, and my music, to create that sound."

His gaze locked into mine as his own passion spoke through his eyes and voice. "In an exceptional orchestra, each player contributes his or her own unique sound. At the same time, the unique sound of each player seamlessly blends with all other sounds to create a unified sound. Uniqueness and unification exist simultaneously, melded together within the passionate love that creates the music. The secret of artful mastery is revealed from within your heart. I am only a guide to help you hear and create from within your heart."

He stayed true to his word, helping each of us, individually and collectively, to listen with greater sensitivity and keenness to the music. A technical response to his questions for improvement had to be accompanied by a suggestion that would deepen the aesthetic sound. But even he did not touch the space that Micaela awakened in me through her sound.

"Is the pot of gold over the rainbow the passionate love the white flame radiated as it hovered over the void? Where did my playful joy go? What is Kokopelli's secret to know such sacred joy? Is it my soul that knew such delight in what appears unimportant to who I am as an adult? Have I been feeling something is missing from within me because my soul has been less present? Such wisdom my soul spoke at my birth. Could that wisdom really be a part of my Being?" The questions were endless, as well as fear and doubt of the unknown.

Thankfully, the house was quiet when I returned, and I went to the kitchen to make hot, herbal tea. I needed something to calm me. When I went to my room, I again looked at Micaela's ballad. I was stunned how its essence echoed what my soul had shared. "How is this possible? Who could this woman be?" Iris was right. Micaela knew me, and she knew her and Ethan. But what, exactly, did she know about us?

I put the ballad on my bedside table and got ready for bed. I decided the best thing to do was to see how Iris and Ethan responded. Perhaps they could help provide an explanation. When the last drops of my comforting tea were sipped, I put my aching head on my soft pillow. Thankfully, I soon fell into a very deep, sound sleep.

SIX

I awoke to the smell of Antonio's special coffee brewing. I would miss his unique presence and touches with his "art" when I moved further away. I recognized my good fortune and never took what I had for granted. On occasion, I invited someone at school, who needed a couple of days away, to stay for a night or two. Having been spared the financial hardships of many, I felt I should act with kindness by sharing my good fortune. With that thought, Micaela's ballad about acting generously toward others to be rewarded by God's favor in the future, resounded through me. Inviting others to ease my guilt was not an act of charity; it was an act of manipulation. "Wow, I've been blind to my motives and agendas. No wonder I couldn't enjoy my company."

I did, however, enjoy witnessing the delight Antonio stirred in people I invited. It was rare to be with an adult who shared pure joy. Antonio once told me that while he loved to cook, sharing his creations gave him the greatest pleasure. He always appreciated the extra people to serve. "Interesting," I thought, "how passion for one's labor flavors it with richness." I realized Antonio shared his creations not out of duty or want, but only to share his joy. "In the future, I'll invite someone not to ease my guilt or any other emotion, but to share the rare joy here."

I wondered what Antonio's secret was. "Perhaps someday soon I'll ask him," I told myself aloud to cement my need to do so. I recognized the profound love I sensed from Micaela as the same love Antonio radiated. Growing used to Antonio's radiant joy over the years, I never grasped how truly profound it was. No wonder so many people knew delight in his company. I put the ballad into my pocket and headed downstairs to claim my coffee. When I got to the kitchen, my mug rested next to the full coffee pot, ready to be poured.

"Morning Antonio," I said through a voice that carried my deep gratitude for his presence.

Antonio turned to look at me, the glimmer in his black eyes covering his entire face with a glow. "You're up quite early. Must be the enticing aroma of my coffee calling you. It's ready to be relished. Another remarkable fall day to be relished as well."

I filled my mug while nodding my agreement, hesitated for a moment as I debated if it was a good time to talk, then decided to head outside to the garden, instead. Right now, I needed to savor his coffee in quiet before sharing the ballad with Ethan and Iris. I sat on the bench opposite the angel to absorb its majesty. This morning, the sky was alive with the pulsating colors of the sunrise reflecting their joyful dance upon the silver of the angel's gown. Its multicolored, shimmering reflection of the sunrise fell upon the rainbow of irises surrounding it. The irises opened to receive this light while blending the vibrations of Earth and sky. The angel's golden crown weaved light through the early morning colors as if to sanctify the garden. Breathing the angel's enchanting allure within, the sun, angel, irises, and myself shared a unified space of sacredness. "I can't let this beauty disappear. No wonder Iris felt incomplete, and Ethan restless and sullen."

Ethan called for me to join them on the deck. His anticipation of what the ballad contained announced itself in his sharply focused eyes. Handing it to him, he placed it on the table between himself and Iris. They were quiet for some time, reading and rereading the words. Ethan mumbled some incomprehensible words now and then. His intense eyes examined each word, his brow squinting to support the intensity of his energy. Iris sat still and quiet, her head slightly nodding in agreement as she read. Droplets, releasing the waters of her sentiments, fell from her eyes, soothing the heated table that was absorbing Ethan's intensity. Iris' only movement was the occasional nod of her head. After some time, she began to talk.

"It's evident Micaela knows us as souled beings. About six months ago, I had a dream that took me back to the time of your birth when I was enveloped in sacred light. A being of light came to me, echoing its loving vibration that at least one spiritual master would be revealed to us soon. This person, or persons, would help us recognize and move through obstacles that blocked our expansion into the sacredness we once shared. The wisdom of Micaela's words tells me she is one of those masters.

"I felt your love when you were born, Dakari, and you've always been an angel of love. The angel in my garden has also become an angel of love, sheltering the sacred words of your soul in its dark, interior chamber. My faith had become a comfort for the limitations I felt in raising you. Finding tolerance and mercy for others, no matter how much they teased the boundaries of what I believed goodness to be, helped me find tolerance for my own limitations. But self-judgment has not left me. The shame and guilt keeping it alive are burrowed so deeply within my cells that the most minuscule traces remaining multiply like an out-of-control virus. Exhaustion, incompleteness, restlessness, gnawing fear do continue to plague me. I recognize my barrier built of fear that prevents my full surrender into the depths of wisdom the dark holds. Perhaps Micaela will help bring resolution to the confusion I've been unable to resolve."

Ethan's attention remained fixed upon the ballad as Iris spoke. "Amazing, simply amazing how Micaela depicted my hope," he said as if talking to himself. "I do try to control my mind, holding disturbing emotions at bay pretending they don't exist. My unacknowledged emotions have been getting in the way of my creativity. Perhaps the hope I've known is merely a trap I created to avoid facing the fallacies I cling to. I've been so blind to the tension that fills my days, always projecting something better into the future. But tomorrow always fills itself with the tensions of today."

Silence returned as we attempted to eat breakfast. The piercing intelligence in Ethan's eyes remained drawn inward as if to search deeply for answers. At one point, he shared that Micaela's words were calling him to examine where the core of his beliefs originated, and his own truth related to them. He mumbled a bit about how his sincere efforts to do so after my birth gave way to routine actions after getting discouraged. I do not know if he was aware he spoke these words aloud because the distant stare in his eyes did not seek acknowledgment of his words.

I imagined my eyes reflected Ethan's empty stare. There was no comfort in having the rug pulled out from the ground that supported who I knew myself to be, and the beliefs I held. Everything was cracked open, and a vacuum created from that crack. I recalled Iris in her garden of my dream, and her panicked fear of the Earth's open void. She could not sense the compassionate light present to support her as she sought support from a

God she could not understand and feel but continued to hold faith in. Would I trust that support was present, or would I panic and shrink in fear? I did not know the answer. But I was willing to override any fear that would keep me from meeting with Micaela.

Before leaving the table to return to my apartment, I shared that I planned to email Micaela when I returned home. Iris asked if I would invite her to the house to meet her and Ethan if he agreed. Ethan nodded his approval. I said I would do so if I felt comfortable with her. They had already left for errands by the time I collected my things to leave, but at the door Antonio was waiting. He handed me a small package wrapped in his traditional rainbow birthday paper and ribbons. My face, wearing a grin of sheer joy, was matched by his eyes glowing in love.

"A little something to acknowledge and celebrate your new adult life. Open it when you return to your apartment."

I thanked him and put it in my backpack. I was about to call for a taxi to the train station when I abruptly stopped in my tracks. "Why was I hurrying to get back to the city, when I really wanted to ask Antonio about the deep contentment that I saw in him? Why not ask now?"

"Do you have time to talk? There are things I'd like to ask about yourself."

"Sure Dakari, I always have time for you. Interested in sitting in the garden? You know I also enjoy that space. But leave your gift here."

I was not surprised to see Antonio sit on the bench next to the angel, although I cannot tell you why. Just an intuitive sense, and my "gut" was at the forefront of my experiences lately. I sat on the bench opposite him. A memory of me as a kid in the garden sitting next to Antonio, right where he now sat, surfaced. "I remember sitting next to you on that bench as a kid, and you talking to me about the garden and the angel."

Antonio nodded his agreement. "Can you recall anything I said and how you felt? Just relax through your breath, clearing any thoughts that might interfere with your recall."

Trusting Antonio, I did as he suggested. I had been focused on the trip back home, dimming the compassion I knew all weekend. But as I stilled my chatter through my breath, it slowly returned. A sensation of warmth surrounding Antonio, myself, and the angel expanded from within. I knew it well; it was the ever-present glow of joy I knew as a young boy. While some of its presence had left me, its glow had not dimmed in Antonio. I vaguely recalled words about my soul Antonio had shared. While the words were unclear, the joyful feeling was crystal clear.

"Ah, so happy to see a warm glow about you," Antonio said while encouraging me to expand deeper into it. "I've missed that beaming presence in you. Clearly, your heart's inner glow is helping you sense what you felt when you were younger. The words are not important. Much more important, and vital, is the awareness that supports your words. I knew when you entered the house this weekend, you had an intense awakening into the light of who You really are. Your eyes were alive with the spark of your spirit."

I was spinning, wondering if I heard Antonio correctly. I looked at him as I had never looked at him before. He, and the angel, glistened in a shared light. I vaguely recalled sharing that magic, so full of endless joy, when I was young. Like Iris and Ethan, Antonio encouraged wonder and awe, never diminishing the joy of my imagination. But my play with Antonio held a magic that was untouched when with others. I looked into Antonio's eyes to express gratitude for what he shared. He turned his sparkling eyes to the angel while inviting me, through the language of his heart, to do the same. The angel's black pupils dilated, calling me to enter their dark depths as it had beckoned me to do before.

"Relax into your breath," I heard Antonio say. "It's all good. I understand your confusion, but you can handle this. You've never fallen completely asleep to your spirit's creativity, even though its presence has dimmed. Trust the angel. It nurtures the flame of your soul that you will slowly own as an essence of You, too."

Surrendering to what the eyes of the angel offered, I lost my sense of place and time. "Do not resist," I heard Antonio's gentle voice say. "Your soul wishes to speak to you."

I vaguely recalled playing with the angel as I entered its eyes through my breath. Within the space of my closed eyes, all was pitch-black, just like the blackness I had experienced as Micaela began to play her violin. "Breathe deeply through love," I heard myself say in silent unison with Antonio's voice. "Breathe deeply through love." My voice increasingly blended with the sacredness I sensed in Antonio's voice, its rich depths resonating all sound frequencies. There was no male or female voice to be differentiated. Ever so slowly, all sound gave way to a sacred silence. Glistening strands of golden light, threaded throughout the radiant darkness of my inner sight, revealed themselves. A luminous oval light appeared from within these golden threads, and I surrendered into the bliss of its touch.

"Dakari, I am your intuitive Self, the divinity of your soul. My loving light touched Iris and Ethan during your birth. You embodied me throughout your childhood, experiencing the world through my magic. As your mind matured, assuming the density that supports logic, I could no longer share the fullness of my magic with you. But my whisper never left you. I'm always soaring about, teasing your intuitive sense that I am yet to be fully present within you and your creations.

"The craftsman for the angel was Antonio. He is a spiritual master who infused the angel's form with my essence, the divine essence of your very own Beingness. Even as a teenager, as you opened Antonio's gifts in the garden, you sensed and received the presence of my pure love. Your mind is familiar with my presence, although its logic doubts me. But I believe it will increasingly absorb my wisdom as its guide, even though it's somewhat resistant to do so now. In time, its known laws of man will be surrendered to work in cooperation with divine law that is not of cause-and-effect reasoning.

"I do not wish to overwhelm your mind with details. But it is important to know that you, Iris, and Ethan have important work on this Earth that cannot be accomplished by your minds alone. None of you will lose your minds, or your memories, but the agendas that now guide you will disappear. It's time to expand your knowing of self beyond your earthly identity. With a quiet, still mind feel the inner depths of my sacredness; it is Your sacredness. Breathe my presence deep within and exhale this sacred breath into your flute. Your human self has only to allow me. Trust my presence just as you trust the joyful presence Antonio shares with you."

I lost all sense of time and do not know how long I sat in the garden. At some point, I heard Antonio's voice calling me to take the thermos of coffee he prepared for my trip back. He had called a cab, and it would be here in about 10 minutes. I clumsily walked to him, took the thermos, gathered my things, and the cab came. Before I left, Antonio asked that I not speak to Ethan and Iris of what was shared. Soon, they would learn who he is. Meeting his bright eyes, I nodded, then left.

SEVEN

It was late afternoon when I got home. I felt more fatigue than usual from the train. Weekday commuters were quietly lost to their phones, but weekend trains were filled with people noisily sharing details of their lives with friends. Their chatter irritated a space that felt unusually sensitive to their voices. I took a hot bath with lavender and rose oils to help unravel tension. The water's warmth and plant essences coaxed my muscles to relax, and my mind to be still. I was glad I bought a sandwich on my way home to enjoy with Antonio's coffee. I needed to relax and listen to music.

As I ate, I listened intently to the melodies the songs sang. When various instruments became the vibrating colors of the rainbow, I knew I was forever changed. Finishing the last remains of my sandwich and coffee,

I remembered my gift. I opened the package carefully, absorbing my awareness of the sacredness the carving held. Protected by black fabric with gold and silver weaved throughout, a miniature-sized replication of the angel in the garden, on its granite pedestal, awaited my embrace. Easing it from its case, its golden crown glistened in the lamp's light. The silver within its eyes reflected its crown's golden light, and its black pupils teased me to venture inward to their depths. Although I did not allow myself to fully enter its black pupils, my mind was relaxing, enabling me to feel their compassion. The flame of its pedestal appeared to pulsate ever so delicately, and the serpents' bodies gracefully pulsated in synchrony with the flame they cradled. I recalled the many comments people made when in the garden about how "elegant" the serpents appeared. I had wondered why no one expressed a learned fear of them. "Perhaps they sensed the deep love I feel without being aware of it. Truth uncovering falsehoods through love," I thought.

I put the silk fabric on my bedside table, resting the angel on it. Its card stated, "At center, the space of infinity, is the divine love that transmutes fear and judgment. Embrace this radiant love through compassionate surrender of what is not your truth. Be the wisdom that does not engage with forces that separate and judge. Create from within, to manifest beauty from without." After adding Antonio's colorful ribbons to the silver ribbon that protected the words of my very own intuitive Self, I placed the silk paper, and the card, at the ivory lotuses of the angel's feet.

I had classwork due tomorrow and tried to find a focus to get it done. Slowly directing my attention to this work, my mind's logic took over. When I glanced at the angel through my "hardened" sight, its form began to lose its magical qualities. It was assuming a static nature as if the vibrations I had sensed never existed. "Do not be deceived through a vision of limitation. Beneath my solid appearance perceived through your human mind, I vibrate with the sacredness of life perceived through your divine mind. My vision is dynamic, not static," it faintly whispered through vibrations that refused to be deadened.

I was thankful when a classmate called with questions about an assignment. While discussing various answers to his questions, my mind settled. A return to its routines comforted it, although an underlying anxiety of what was ahead made itself known when my work was done. Perhaps to distract my mind's apprehension of the future, I emailed Micaela about possible times and places to meet. She responded saying that Friday, at a small café I suggested in Little Italy, was good for her. She suggested we have pizza as well, and I confirmed dinner. Everything was in motion, spinning within my entire body as I rested my head on my pillow and fell into a sound sleep.

Friday night finally arrived. It had been the most intense week of my life and focusing on my work was not easily achieved. Before practicing my flute, I breathed as much love as I could allow within me, clearing my mind's chatter. Most times, I found some degree of calm, although my mind's chatter was never far off. It had grown accustomed to accepting that nature was alive with conscious awareness and light devas living within it. But my mind understood nature's awareness as separate from it. The idea that nature's wisdom was an essence of my Beingness, to be in a cooperative relationship with, was not something it willingly accepted. After all, this idea posed a great threat to the autonomous authority and control it was accustomed to.

"You have an extraordinarily vivid imagination that I've been willing to go along with," my mind voiced one day as it penetrated through my calm. "Ethan and Iris were at a breaking point at your birth and were hallucinating. While Ethan benefited financially, and in his professional status, Iris had been left with confusion. Revisiting that time has created confusion even in Ethan now, threatening his past gains to explore mere fantasy. Substantial loss could come to you, also, if you give truth to fantasy. Antonio has agendas outside of your interest. He manipulated you with his powerful suggestions, making what was unreal, appear real. Do not be a fool to trust him or Micaela."

How much weight these thoughts carried varied from

day to day. I had experienced a love whose sacredness felt beyond manipulation. How could I have imagined such majestic beauty? Antonio and Micaela radiated profound love and creativity, and I was willing to give them a chance despite my doubts and fears. Even Iris and Ethan sensed Micaela's wisdom. Although unacknowledged, I believed they sensed Antonio's wisdom as well. As a treasured part of the family, they never took his presence for granted.

I was at the café a little early, but Micaela was already there. She greeted me as if she had always known me, putting me in an unusual state of ease. As I took my jacket off, the waiter came with pizza and salad. Smelling its enticing aroma, I realized how hungry I was and did not hesitate to help myself. Micaela did the same.

"When you suggested this café, I thought of how much I enjoy their pizza. I'd be eating by myself if you didn't agree to join me. I'm glad to have your company."

I nodded as I bit into my food. We shared light conversation as we ate, mostly about our love for music. At some point, I told her where I went to college, and my passion to create music that sang as her voice and violin did. "I've been searching for something that's missing from within me, and the music I create. When I heard you play, I knew you held some answers for me. Nothing about my life has been the same since last Friday."

"I didn't know the exact nature of your vision as I played, but I knew you were allowing my music to deeply penetrate the space where your sacredness is seated. The thoughts of most people are heavy with fear and judgment. The subtle, pure resonance that master artists create through touches and soothes those burdened with deep, emotional wounds of their human heart. But the powerful, majestic presence of divine passion and understanding are unknown to the mind. Feeling threatened by its presence, the mind generates emotions of fear and distrust that block its entry. I felt your mind's fear and distress as I played, but I also saw you allowing light to assist you. It's evident your mind knows this light but doubts its potential."

As Micaela spoke, I re-experienced the radiance of that light. Its presence stirred a fiery passion in my belly that filled every cell of my being. My rising passion felt explosive, and words flowed from me that shared the details of my dream as she played. Everything, except the soothing warmth of her green eyes, was lost to me. At one point, the green hues in her eyes took the form of a soothing flame. Its healing glow calmed my mind's demanding voice not to accept my vision as real. The last words I spoke described the compassion that remained with me over much of the weekend. I did not share later events.

"Very beautiful. Your intuitive imagination hasn't been completely deadened as it has in most people. True creativity echoes depthless, sacred vibrations. It's not sourced from, or contained within, the human mind and heart. It lies deep within the dark, ethereal waters of our intuitive, divine mind and heart that are not of time as we know it to be. As young children, we were unified within the essence of this loving passion. Being of the divine mind and heart, our breath freely flowed within its subtle dimensions. We imagined through this sacredness and played with other light beings and nature devas. But as we matured, our minds grew in complexity while absorbing the charged thoughts of others. Open space compressed itself into the density of measured time. This dense space was the perfect environment for the maturing logic of the mind to support its reason and charged emotions.

"The mind of logic rejects an intelligence that exists outside its known boundaries of measured time and space. It knows a separation between it and everything else. Its established beliefs and judgments dictate how the world is known and acted upon. The sacred, malleable reality we once knew as children is lost to a conditioned reality that is unchanging and unbending. Every quality has its opposite to be analyzed and judged: male and female, human and god, good and evil, and so forth. Judgments become a cement wall as our charged thoughts are relentlessly recycled. Our breath, limited to the dense space of our charged thoughts, becomes shallow and impure. Any change that threatens the fortress of our mind's beliefs is deeply feared, strengthening its walls of resistance."

I nodded, even though I felt overwhelmed by her

words. But she had confirmed my suspicion that the tools of science were limited to what the mind could perceive and investigate. Such passion was present in her voice and eyes, and it was this passion that touched me within a space that was not of my mind. Before I knew it, words again flew from my mouth. "Feeling into my heart has always been my focus when creating music. But now, I'm beginning to grasp that the heart of my sacred Self holds true passion, not my human heart. I was trying to force what can't be forced. I need to follow this path. I can't settle for mediocrity and know contentment. But I feel my mind's fearful resistance. It can't accept what I feel through my imagination as anything other than pure fantasy that can't be trusted."

Micaela nodded slightly, her compassionate eyes acknowledging my words. Perhaps, to avoid further conversation that was beyond my capacity to understand, I asked if she knew I would be at the café.

"I trust and listen to the guidance of my intuitive sense. It's the voice of my divine soul. When I sense I need to be at a specific place to perform, I show up. I allow wisdom's synchronicity to manage the details of others. Even the words to my songs are conceived through my intuitive sense of what others need to hear. The inner, intuitive waters of each person were stirred by my song, although most minds will later reject nudges that tease change. We create what's in our lives by the energies we call to us. Your desire to awaken into your spirit's deepest passion led you to me. Your mind sensed danger as you pondered whether to come in, and you almost listened to it. My ballad's title was far from agreeable to it."

I chuckled in agreement. But I did not stop there. The details of the past weekend flowed from me. All of them, including the words I sensed my soul shared, how Iris and Ethan experienced my birth, and the angel Antonio had infused my soul's essence into. Micaela stopped me just once to ask what I wanted for dessert as the waiter cleared the table. She listened through a silent calm of acceptance. I took occasional short breaks to sip my cappuccino and eat dessert, avoiding eye contact when I did so. I needed breaks from the intensity of her listening. She sat quietly, never interrupting my flow, even when I was quiet. "It's odd," I thought as I ate during a break. "I hear Micaela's silent support more than any verbal support from others. Her compassionate silence encourages me to speak through the same space she listens from while lifting my fears. Even silence is filled with vibration, and Micaela radiates a silence that vibrates with sacredness."

"You're experiencing an awakening on a deep level," Micaela said, breaking through my musing. "Know you're prepared to handle this transformation. In fact, you're doing quite well. You've had much support to prepare you for this time. I know Antonio well, although we haven't spoken for a couple of weeks or so. He has told me about you, and I sensed you were the Dakari he knew when your table companions toasted you."

Feeling exhausted, I glanced at the time. Over two hours had passed. It was time to go. I shared the invitation of Iris and Ethan, mentioning that Antonio would be cooking. Micaela smiled and said she was looking forward to it. Email the details, and she would be there. "Antonio knows my favorite foods, so perhaps he could suggest the dinner menu if you send him a message that you met with me, and I'll be the guest. I'd like to talk to Antonio to learn more about Iris and Ethan. Perhaps he would be willing to ask them for permission to do so."

I said I would relay her message, then excused myself to use the restroom. When I returned, she had paid the bill and left. "She's almost invisible the way she comes and goes," I thought. As with last Friday night, I was grateful for the cool air and a comfortable bed to lay my exhausted head on. Before nodding off, I looked at the angel. It seemed to want to talk to me, but I was too exhausted to work with its intense energy. I turned the light off and fell asleep.

EIGHT

"Interesting," I thought one day, "how words that had carried the power to panic me when I first heard them have seeped within, churning my insides upside down. They challenged almost every truth I was taught and had accepted. I suppose that's exactly why panic initially rang through every fiber of my being when I heard them." The words of my soul at my birth, and what others shared, put my mind on the edge of a razor-sharp knife that wanted to scrutinize them. But unlike my mind, my intuitive sense understood that dissecting them would remove the pure inspiration the words spoke. I had to allow the words to sing their sacred vibrations within the space of my divine heart to know them. And my divine heart, I was learning, was a space of sacred silence emptied of charged emotions that included my mind's fear and agendas.

While the progressive art schools I had attended emphasized creativity over rote learning, the brain was always credited as the architect of creativity. Even my orchestra conductor, who emphasized creating music by listening through the heart, had addressed areas within the brain where various elements of music were processed, and the "embedded" musical ability of some brains. Now I knew no scientific measures could validate the passionate love I felt. There was only the sensation of the sacred, and its whispers of wisdom deep within.

As I was getting my flute to practice, the carving of Kokopelli that Antonio had gifted me on my sixth birthday caught my eye. Its card read, "The master flutist is seeded within you. Breathe its sacred notes of inspiration through your flute." I recalled the exact words I said to Antonio when I embraced Kokopelli.

"He looks like me, but my back isn't bent like a rainbow."

"Your back isn't arched like that, but it can carry the rainbow's magic his back carries."

I imagined my eyes lit up at the possibility of my back holding the magic of a rainbow. "How do I make the rainbow come alive in me?"

"You already hold the beauty of the rainbow within you, but its magic will dim as your body and mind mature. I believe when you are ready to reawaken to the rainbow's essence as an adult, you will glow with its magic. For now, just be with the sacred energy the figure holds and enjoy his presence. He breathes sacredness through his flute, and if you stay focused and aware within your own sacredness, you will do the same."

"Does he have a name?"

"His name isn't important now. You'll know who he is when it's time for you to know. The energy he carries is profoundly pure, and you'll need to prepare yourself to receive and embody this sacred presence when you're older."

Antonio was right. I did lose that magic, and it was the loss of that magic that created the always present, nagging question, "What is missing from me, and the music I create? Am I really willing to take steps to receive and embody my sacred energies?" I asked myself as I delicately touched Kokopelli. Looking at the other carvings, a sense of reverence filled me. I watered the lily plant that radiated their peaceful presence while embracing the water as sacred. It nurtured spirit's potentials that were awaiting their time to be touched by my purified breath and brought forward into time through it. I imagined the light within the dark waters infusing itself into my blood, transmuting energies that suffocated the passion wishing to flow through me. I recalled Iris speaking about preparing her inner soil to re-experience the sacredness of my birth. My own mystical awakening was teaching me what it was teaching Iris, arousing compassion for the inner journey she and Ethan had ventured upon as they raised me.

I was better able to focus on my work this week, although with almost everything I did, I sensed a reality deeper than what my mind could know. And that understanding most often led to discomfort. For example, during my Philosophy of Religion class there was a discussion about the tendency for religions to deny people sensuous pleasure. Sensuality aroused and encouraged our subconscious, impulsive instincts and was sinful.

"Do you believe religions suppress parts of our expression, and if so, did a justification exist for that suppression?" the professor asked.

Almost everyone believed there was an element of suppression, but while it was far too extreme, some control was justified. The mind was tempted by its instinctual impulses, and if standards of morality were not explicitly stated and enforced, society could be less moral and safe.

"If we better understood the source of our undesirable impulses, could we temper them without an outside authority needing to tell us what is right and wrong?" he asked.

Most felt that even if the source of our impulses was understood, they were powerful, and reason was easily pushed to the wayside when they arose. Most times, we are not even aware of these impulses. One person said clear standards of morality created shame and guilt when someone acted contrary to them, making them powerful deterrents to immoral behavior. But many objected to inciting these feelings to control behavior, saying they were just as detrimental to our welfare as an unlawful society. However, all recognized that guilt and shame were present in them to some degree. Because these emotions did temper their actions, most were undecided if they did more harm than good.

As I listened to the discussion, my discomfort grew. I recalled Micaela's ballad, sharing her tale of consequences for empowering an external God as the creator and judge of morality. Our inner demons were transformed by acknowledging and accepting them. The divine mind and heart were free of entanglement with, and judgment toward, oppositional forces. I recalled Iris' frustration at how even a trace of judgment became an out-of-control virus that spread through her, fueling shame and guilt for her perceived sins. I envisioned the veil between my human mind and divine mind becoming more and more clogged with toxins as people spoke. Feeling nauseous, I breathed ever more deeply while inviting the compassionate presence of my soul to dissolve the heaviness. I lowered my gaze to shut out the environment.

An image of myself in the garden, dancing with Antonio when I was four or five, entered my inner vision. Antonio suggested we take a break and sit on the bench next to the angel. The angel spoke to me after I sat. "Your dance was such a beautiful creation to participate in. Such great joy to experience dancing on Earth. Always feel this joy, Dakari. It is your joy as your divine Self breathing through you as You. I am always present. You simply need to allow me."

"Dakari," I heard the professor say, "are you feeling alright? You look pale and distracted."

I slowly brought my attention back into the classroom. "I was feeling nauseous, but I'm better now. Everything felt so heavy with gloom. Is it possible that how we're thinking about divinity is flawed? It doesn't feel correct to embrace a divine essence as an authoritative figure who limits and controls sensuality through emotions like shame and guilt. I want my music to be sensuous, to touch people so deeply that they come alive in a love that lifts them from their hardened minds and wounded hearts. Isn't pure beauty sensuous at its core, allowing us to feel ecstatically alive in love? Doesn't this divinity radiate loving, creative passion, not guilt and shame? Life's creative impulses may be wild and undomesticated, but I don't believe they're sinful and corrupt."

The professor shook his head slightly as he pondered what I said. Others started to chime in, rethinking what sensuality and divinity really were, and if they were related. While the comments varied, they stirred some to question their beliefs. Right before class ended, the professor shared that he worked at this college because he loved the Arts. "When I go to concerts and museums sharing your artwork, I'm 'lifted' from my mind's worries and concerns. Art reminds me that beauty does indeed exist. It's not my job to tell you what divinity is or is not. But it is my job to open your minds and hearts to all possibilities in how you know and experience divinity. Thanks, Dakari, for your contribution."

I nodded, anxious to leave the classroom. I preferred keeping my opinions to myself, but I had to speak up to clear the stifling air. I sighed, knowing life was changing on many levels, and I would have to adjust to a new flow with it. I knew this flow could not be dictated by my mind. The imagination that was of my sacred Self had to be the primary life force flowing through me and into my creations, even though I felt quite clueless how to bring this transformation about.

I was glad when classes ended Friday. I had worked feverishly all week to complete my assignments. I wanted my weekend to be free. I did not know where it would take me, but I wanted to delve deeper into my core with Micaela and Antonio to know the sacredness I believed they embodied.

I slept until mid-morning on Saturday, which was unusual for me. But then again, the past two weeks had been the most intense time of my life, and my mind and body were exhausted from these energies. Extra rest was needed. When I recalled Micaela was going to join us for dinner in Westchester tonight, I felt both excitement and apprehension. I had texted Antonio that I met with Micaela, detailing all her suggestions. Trusting Antonio, I knew Ethan and Iris would not object to him speaking with Micaela about them, and that he would have the perfect creation to appease the palates of all. I wondered if Antonio said anything to them about the angel.

It was around three in the afternoon when I arrived. Everyone was busy in the kitchen preparing the meal. Ethan said a quick hello as he turned away from the eggplant he was cutting. Iris was at the stove stirring what smelled to be an Italian sauce but put the spoon down to give me a quick hug, accompanied with her usual loving greeting. Antonio looked away from the lettuce he was rinsing with a huge grin when I greeted him with my spontaneous voice of joy. I noticed cheeses softening on the counter.

"Eggplant parmesan and salad for dinner?"

"You read the clues well. When Antonio relayed Micaela's message, he said eggplant was one of her favorite foods, and we also enjoy it."

"Need any help?"

"I believe it's all under control. There aren't many days like this left before winter sets in. Enjoy the day and the quiet as you wish. Micaela will be here early evening," Iris said.

"I'll do exactly that."

After a needed nap, I headed to the garden. It was cool, too cool to eat outside on the deck, but warm enough to enjoy the air, especially with the sun still out. The songs of the birds were nearly gone, having left for their yearly migration to warmer weather. I missed their joy-filled songs during winter. But Iris knew she could appreciate greater beauty in their songs when they returned if she released what no longer served her inner beauty in their absence.

The flowers and most of the leaves had already surrendered their life force. Their decaying life was nourishing the soil before the onset of winter's freeze. I had studied the mythology of Greek gods and recalled the powerful lightning rod of the god, Zeus. Zeus could be self-righteous and inflexible if he served his own agendas, rather than the greater good. He ruled best when he allowed what no longer served the greater good to be disbanded. In doing so, new ideas could emerge that would better serve all. "The strong winter winds must be the breath of Zeus blazing the fullness of his matured creations prior to parting with the beliefs supporting them. Life yielding to death, death yielding to renewed life. It's the cycle of nature's wisdom completely blended with the divine wisdom that created and supported its life force. It's the wisdom I want to be fully present within, and I'm willing to disband any beliefs that limit my creativity."

Before I knew it, I heard the voices of Micaela and Iris walking to the garden. I greeted Micaela, happy to see her. The few birds remaining in the garden chirped loudly while flying about her as if to acknowledge someone they resonated with.

"When the birds behave like this, I know the person is remarkably special. I rarely see birds excited with a guest," Iris said as she watched the birds.

The angel immediately caught Micaela's eyes, and she went closer to it. I could not see her eyes, but I felt them pierce every detail of its frame. My own body felt pierced with a sacred, vibrating presence. Noticing the flame within the angel's black pedestal glowing, I softened my senses to receive its inviting glow. It stirred a passion just above my navel that spread its fire throughout my entire body. Feeling dizzy, I sat on the bench opposite the angel, finding Iris already there, her eyes closed.

As I breathed deeply, my eyes also closed, and I allowed this sacredness to pulsate through me. The angel's black pupils appeared to my inner vision, then blended into one black eye at the space centered slightly above my two eyes. I had heard this space referred to as the "third eye" that is of wisdom. Once joined, two serpents appeared from within this black fabric. Their bodies expanded and contracted in rhythmic synchrony with the breath flowing through them. It was the rhythm of a river's flow gracefully accommodating its form to the changing space that contained it. Shimmering threads of silver in one serpent, and gold in the other, pulsed within their bodies. The rhythm of the serpents' pulsing breath became the rhythm of my pulsing breath.

"Keep breathing, freeing your breath of resistance as you blend it with the serpents' breath," the angel shared. "The silver threads are eating decay within your cells that have supported the ground of your beliefs and identity. This life force is the shadow of your conditioning that needs to be compassionately embraced to be resolved. The golden threads are seeding the passion of your sacred truth, free of entanglement with the forces of opposition. Breathe the compassion of me, your intuitive Self, deep within. Allow my love to transmute the dense, decaying matter that blocks your inner sacredness. Within your center's core, where creation's vibrations do not exist, all facets of your Beingness will be integrated. Your monsters dissolve when you understand them as your greatest teachers. I am always present, but you must allow my presence to be you, too. Nurture my presence within you, and you will nurture all facets of your Beingness. The roots of Self-love are of the still, cosmic sea within."

Slowly, gradually, the serpents, and their gold and silver threads, dissipated into the blackness of the angel's pupils. Its pupils then blended their separate forms within the dark space behind my closed eyes. A deeply compassionate, translucent light filled the dark void. I heard Ethan's voice telling us dinner was ready. Walking to the house, our laughter from the birds following us helped to ground my awareness back into my body.

NINE

D inner was relaxed and casual. They were as comfortable with Micaela as I was. They shared how deeply her ballad had spoken to them. Iris added her sense that Micaela knew them, and the ballad was written, at least in part, for them. Before Micaela had time to reply, Iris began to share sacred memories of my birth with Ethan adding his experiences at different points. The dining room, always filled with loud chatter when guests were here, was blanketed in a soft calm. Freed of my inner chatter, I was hearing the story of my birth as if it was the first time. They also shared some of their efforts to re-experience the love they felt as it had begun to dim. When they talked themselves out, the compassionate silence the room spoke soothed the lingering vibrations of their voices. I had attributed Micaela's music to my "lifted" state of being, but I now understood her presence was primary to the deep compassion I experienced. Her music merely sang the sacredness she infused into it.

"My intuition guides what my music becomes. I trust those who hear it are called to it because change is calling to them," Micaela said while looking at Ethan and Iris. "But few are moved as deeply as you have been, especially because you didn't hear me sing the words. You allowed the resonance my ballad's words hold to penetrate you, rekindling the beauty you touched at Dakari's birth. I know your bliss, your fears, and your frustrations. All who venture on the inner journey, where profound, sacred energies are touched, can share the bliss you knew and the heartache that followed. I've added new verses to the ballad and would like to sing them before we talk more. I believe it will help you understand your frustrations with your efforts. Does that sound good?"

We voiced our unanimous agreement.

"Do you need a violin?" Ethan asked.

"Yes, but I'll warm it up myself while we sit here."

"Sure, I'll get my favorite violin."

"You may want to record my ballad to listen to it again."

Ethan nodded his agreement as he walked away.

Antonio joined us for dinner as he sometimes did.

He had cleared the table so unobtrusively I was surprised to see the dishes gone when the conversation ended. Only water was left sitting on the table.

Ethan returned, putting his recorder down before handing his violin to Micaela. His reverent manner illustrated his wish for every filament of her presence to meld into his violin. I understood. I wanted her resonance singing through my flute, too. Micaela gracefully embraced Ethan's violin, resting it upon her shoulder as a parent tenderly rested a newborn. Her warmup began. I watched Ethan's eyes brighten, seeming to recognize the purity of sound that touched him 21 years ago.

"Beautiful, absolutely beautiful," he quietly murmured.

Ethan's violin began to sing as it had never sung before. The clarity in her notes pierced my being. From within the translucent darkness of my third eye, the calming waters of the vortex appeared, along with the white flame that hovered above it. I breathed the flame's passion, now soothed by the water, into my depths. The movement of the buoyant saltwater felt guided by a pulsing flow of immense love within it, and it radiated joy. Allowing the water's pulsing joy to blend with the pulsing flow of my blood, I was enveloped in bliss. Slowly, and with immense love that knew no resistance, the water surrendered into the darkness of the vortex. My bliss mellowed any fear of entering the vortex with the water.

Only the flame now occupied the translucent

darkness of space. Opening to receive the depths of its passion through my breath, the movement of my breath became the flowing movement of a bird's illuminated wings. As my breath, these wings effortlessly expanded and contracted while emitting the sacred vibrations of free-flowing grace. Then, in a blaze of sublime, white light, the flame diffused its form within the darkness of space. Nothing was present to be distinguished: no dimensions, no forms, no attributes. Yet, the darkness was passionately alive as an echo of loving wisdom.

The magnitude of this wisdom was beyond what I was prepared to merge with, and I sensed panic awaiting its moment to strike me down into density. Thankfully, Micaela's music ended, and the touch of Antonio's presence guided my awareness back into my body from the sacred dimensions I had expanded into. I vaguely recalled this sensation as a kid when I shared magical realms with him. "He was always there assisting me," I realized. "Such immense beauty. Everything pales to what I now feel."

We sat in silence for a few moments, until Micaela spoke the title to her revised ballad: "Freeing Hope, Faith, and Love from Enslavement". After playing a few more notes, she began to sing without the violin.

> The angel of faith embraced her holiness from within.
> Her shameful, buried misdeeds, she would concede.
> The release through compassion, her inner divinity
>   would light,

The decayed life within, her inner divinity would
   wash away.
Her attunement to indwelling grace sets her free of
   judgment's feed.

Releasing mind control unveiled her doubt and
   mistrust.
Creating space for the fullness of the moment to
   show.
Exhaustion, incompleteness, restlessness, gnawing
   fear:
The angel of faith embraced all through love that
   would grow.

The angel of hope embraced his liberation from
   within.
The hopelessness he had fled, he no longer would
   dread.
The building of renewed structures, his inner divinity
   would light,
The need for resolute force, his inner divinity would
   wash away.
His surrender to indwelling wisdom sets him free
   from his head.

Releasing mind control unveiled his fear and despair,
Preparing space for the fullness of the moment to
   show.
Exhaustion, incompleteness, restlessness, gnawing
   fear:
The angel of hope embraced all through love that
   would grow.

The angel of love embraced his creativity from
   within.

For inspiration bathed in compassion, he would
yield his say.
The searing flame of Self-love, his inner divinity
would light.
The negation of Self-care, his inner divinity would
carry away.
His surrender to indwelling love sets him free of
culture's way.

Releasing mind control unveiled his motives and
needs.
Creating space for the fullness of the moment to
show.
Exhaustion, incompleteness, restlessness, gnawing
fear:
The angel of love embraced all through love that
would grow.

We are the angels of hope, faith, and love . . .
Claiming our inner divinity that frees us from
despair, fear, and pain.
Faith, the yield to the inner movement of wisdom's
flow, we will embrace.
Hope, the promise of spirit's imagery carried forth
into time, we will breathe.
Divine love, the nectar that resolves entanglement
with opposites, we will sense.
Spirit's passion, bathed in intuitive waters of
love, will be our guiding flame.

Silence fell, except for the deepened hum of
compassion filling the room's space. It was Ethan's voice,
full in pure love, that brought me back into the space of

the room and the distinct physical forms that occupied it. When I saw subtle waves of light energy vibrate through the room's space, I knew I was seeing through more than my physical eyes alone; I was also perceiving through the eyes of my soul Self. Iris was quietly shedding tears.

"I now feel what I chose to leave behind. I don't want to get lost again." Ethan's eyes closed after he spoke, his body unusually still. I knew he wanted to be with the sacredness he sensed.

After some time, Micaela's voice seamlessly entered the tranquil silence. "In your deep state of panic during Dakari's birth, a void of sacredness opened from deep within your being, igniting the spark of your spirit's passionate, creative flame. Through your expanded awareness, you sensed sound as your spirit senses sound. But your mind and body were unprepared to absorb the magnitude of loving passion the music embodied. So, your awareness gradually contracted back into the habituated sound patterns of your rational mind."

Ethan nodded as his eyes turned inward. Then he began to talk. "My time in the garden when Dakari was young helped to keep that sacred passion alive to some degree. But when he grew into an adolescent and I visited the garden less, it was increasingly difficult to imagine the pure sound I knew at his birth."

When he paused, Micaela suggested we drink water to ground ourselves back into our bodies. After some time, Ethan again began to speak from a faraway space.

Like Iris and me, he was not fully present in his body despite the water.

"I've been feeling so much tension as I forcefully attempted to keep my hope alive that these sacred vibrations would magically return. The peace I now feel is free of tension. If I allowed it, my calm would leave. No wonder I was running around in circles."

"Your tension is your mind's desire to keep things as they are when you've intuitively recognized the necessity for change. Your growing tendency to analyze and judge sound quality through your mind's logic, separated from your intuition, has also created tension. Losing trust in your intuition to guide you, your music merely recycled the known into a slightly different pattern. True creativity unfolds from a timeless space within, pulsating with sacredness as it flows forward into time. Its imagery embodies depthless inspiration and cannot be analyzed; it can only be extended. Spirit's essence cannot dance with a vibration that is of linear time and its plotted data points. It's your spirit's passion, not your mind's analysis and emotions, that guides music sourced from within your sacred depths. Spirit's passion lacks nothing. Its imagery is complete unto itself. Feel its presence while receiving its inspiration deep within your being, then bring its pure resonance forth through your music.

"The natural order of life is to release the old into the void to be renewed with a life of extended sacredness. You must choose to serve your ego and its accolades, or to serve life's wisdom that seeks only to extend its creativity. Listen to the ballad often while breathing its sacredness through you. Your mind will create tension from its fear of the unknown. Acknowledge and accept this tension but don't get entangled with it and attempt to control it. If you do, the tension will return with greater intensity. The passionate love infused into the music will transmute your tension if you allow its presence to open space within you. Please, don't try to replicate my sound. Your spirit sings its own unique song through you, and you want to open to receive and integrate its song as it blends with all parts of your beingness.

"My mind, too, had to accept that great beauty is sourced from a timeless dimension that is of your spirit's passion, not of its logic. Ever so slowly, my mind allowed this loving passion to flow through me while serving this grace by giving it form through my music. This act of Self-love continues to extend my inner depths while also extending the creativity of life itself. Find stillness in the holy, cosmic sea of your intuitive Self, your divine mind within, where the passion of your spirit resides. Birth children of hope that radiate divine beauty. Inspire others to unveil their inner beauty through your sacred creations."

Ethan nodded ever so slightly. Antonio suggested we take a break to have dessert, and all agreed. As we ate, Micaela humored us with a story about herself as a young adult who gave complete authority to her mind and its emotions. "Oh, the drama I once created!" she said through a soft chuckle. "My music wasn't worth listening to, but it took me some time to admit my limitations and make the commitment to real change."

Even Ethan laughed quietly, then humored us with a story about how he reacted to praise from a famous musician. "He was using flattery to get work from me. Relishing the praise, I ate the bait. I doubt that will happen again. I'm grateful for your suggestion to tape your music. I'm also glad I didn't think to turn the recorder off when you finished singing. I need to listen to your music, and your words, repeatedly."

"I'll be listening with you, Ethan," Iris said, then shifted her gaze to Micaela. "When you looked at the angel in the garden, it embraced me with its light-filled wings as it has done many times in my dreams, lifting me into a sacred space. Its message, full in love, remains etched into the fibers of my being. I will share my intuitive sense of its words. 'Feel this sacredness. Breathe this sacredness. It lacks nothing. It seeks nothing. It is complete unto itself. Stop seeking a God external to you. Your timeless, sacred depths are unveiled from within, not from without. You act through faith when you yield to the inner movement of life's creative process and remain attuned to its creative source.'

"As you played the violin and sang, the angel's form appeared, radiating its compassion. I sensed the same words being shared, but its light penetrated even deeper. It left, dimming the compassion that had filled space. I saw myself in my garden, breaking the Earth's frozen surface to plant iris seeds. I was sad because I knew I'd again be left with the shame and guilt I sought to release. I sensed the angel's presence, directing me to breathe Earth's sacredness through my mind and body.

Standing still, I anchored my feet and shovel into the ground and breathed its sacredness. My calming breath enabled the softening of my brittle, concrete wall of resistance while transforming it into porous, soft cheese. My shovel began to glow, becoming a wooden scepter with a silver and gold ball at its top. 'My scepter knows no force, only love of Self,' the angel whispered through the breeze. 'This love is your sacred center, Iris, uncluttered with emotions that include shame and guilt. At center, all judgments of duality are balanced in a love that transcends oppositional tensions. Only the compassionate love of your sacred Self that my scepter symbolizes can thaw the frozen, hardened barrier of your mind. True surrender is through love, never through force.'

"When I no longer sensed the angel's vibrations, I saw you carving the angel," she said while looking at Antonio. "The oval light of Dakari's soul from his birth was filling the angel's hollow center. I understood you to be a spiritual master who infused the angel with Dakari's soul. Right before my vision left, the angel showed my body beginning to fill with the colors of the rainbow. 'The rainbow body is the body that does not empower charged emotions,' the angel said. 'The most subtle vibrations of creation exist within you as You. There is so much waiting for you. You have only to allow this sacredness.'"

"Yes, I sculpted the angel," Antonia said when Iris stopped speaking, "and I did infuse the angel with Dakari's soul essence. But much is changing now."

"I sensed that change this week as I washed the angel yesterday while you were in the kitchen. Laying my hands on its opened palms, its compassion flowed from them and into mine. It was the compassion I felt at Dakari's birth and in my dreams when the angel embraced me. I sensed an invitation to fill its open palms with my own light."

"You've been preparing your inner soil to receive your soul's grace since Dakari's birth," Micaela said. "Like Ethan, you were more attuned to the compassion you felt at his birth and when he was young, infusing the outer and inner soil of your garden with it. But as your awareness touched sacred realms, your mind's demons, with their insistent critical chatter, stirred chaos within you. Empowering them through fear, you got stuck in your wounded, human heart. Its love is entangled with pain and suffering that grows in intensity as agitations are recycled. In your work you act different characters, but your worn-out story of suffering remains infused within them. The great majority of gods and goddesses do continue to play out their inner battles and suffer from their actions. But you can practice being a witness to their suffering, just as you can practice being a witness to your own suffering.

"The sacred love you now feel is breathing through your wounded human heart, dissolving its wounds. Nature is infused with this sacred love, and it's this love that you want to nourish your inner and outer gardens with. Imagine the seeds planted in your gardens infused with the essence you now feel. True faith is a process of sensing and embodying the loving passion of your intuitive Self and spirit. To trust wisdom and merge with its free-flowing breath is to embody the creative process of life itself. Attune to the realm of your sacred imagination. Your inner and outer gardens will radiate beauty.

"It's getting late, and there's been much shared to be digested. Dakari, I sense you heard what needed to be heard. Am I correct?"

"Agreed. It's helping to clarify what you said a week ago."

"Expanding into your inner depths is a slow, gradual process as understanding and trust between all facets of your Beingness evolve over time. Antonio has prepared all of you, to varying degrees, to receive and absorb the potent radiance of your inner divinity." Looking at Ethan and Iris she continued, "Both of you needed to experience the futility of relying solely on your mind to bring you peace all these years. Antonio's presence has helped the whisper of your sacred Self stay alive, keeping you from completely sinking into the thick fear most human minds share and perpetuate. Only the radiance of your inner divinity can transmute the fear of your mind, and its debilitating actions and reactions in relationship with self and others. But you needed to be willing to acknowledge my words.

"How about we meet in another four or five weeks? The time will give needed space for absorption of what we shared. I have Dakari's email and will send possible places, times, and dates in a week or so."

As they left, Antonio asked that he not be treated any differently. While we assured him his wish would be honored, I knew it was impossible to do. I was fully aware of my deepened respect and love for his presence.

TEN

We all slept in on Sunday morning. Even nature was silent as rain soaked its body that was preparing for winter hibernation. Listening intently to the sound of heavy water droplets reaching and borrowing into Earth's surface, I felt it soothe the sun's passionate fire that had mercilessly penetrated its body all summer. I vaguely recalled Antonio talking to me after an intensely dry, hot summer that scorched the garden, despite Iris' efforts to keep the flowers from dying. "The sun's passion to manifest a renewed reflection of its beauty on Earth, by burning the old, is not something humans can control or contain. The burning passion Earth has absorbed will be nurtured and prepared for renewed life in the stillness of Earth's winter body. In the spring and summer, Earth will again radiate its magnificence as vibrant flowers. Sometimes, extraordinary passion is necessary to burn the old for the new to be birthed."

"At times, the burning seems anguishing," I thought, "especially when new seeds seem to take forever to gestate. But I embrace my despair and accept all challenges that must be faced and moved through to unveil my deepest inner majesty. I will allow only my spirit's inspiration as seeds of my musical creations. I will still my thoughts, feel my soul's sacred, loving vibrations hovering about me, and absorb them into my being through my breath."

When I finally ventured downstairs, Iris was making coffee. She said Ethan went for breakfast and would return any moment. We sat with our coffee in the sunroom. "Strange," Iris said, "how I always see a subtle rainbow glow over Antonio's carvings, even on days like today when the sun's rays are completely hidden. Believing I was imagining this glow, I never acknowledged its beauty. I'll no longer diminish my imagination as a trick of my mind. I'll relate to it as the light of my spirit's inspiration eternally blazing from within. All this time, Antonio's grace was showing itself, but I never acknowledged it. No wonder I always waited until he was here to clean the angel. I was cleansing its surface dirt with soapy water, but Antonio was cleansing the toxins it absorbed from us with his compassion. The angel's glow that appeared as I cleansed it became visible after I was cleansed of heavy emotions. Only then, could it reflect my glow. How different I see things now."

"I've always noticed how everyone loves Antonio," I said. "He ignites joy in people. I'm beginning to recall memories of my time with him as a kid. My play was filled with deep magic. It feels awkward to accept this magic as a part of me, but I can't ignore the profound beauty I've been feeling. It was 'me' for most of my life. I just got lost in my mind for a while, believing its thoughts defined who I am. I can understand why my mind feels so resistant to allow a presence that isn't fear-based."

We sat quietly, enjoying the subtle glow of the rainbow over the carvings. It reminded me of my dream in the garden, and I shared it with her. She nodded at times, seeming to connect with its imagery.

"Ethan and I talked for some time last night before finally falling asleep. I was caught in a web of shame and guilt, empowering their taunting judgment that kept me from releasing what fueled their own life force. They fed off my self-judgment, inflaming exactly what I thought I wanted to let go of. Now I understand my shame and guilt remained only because unconsciously, I wanted them to remain. They were the reality my mind knew, and I had lived mainly in my mind for most of my life. I understand my panic in your dream. There *is* a void of the unknown that's being created as I begin to embrace my soul's love, and not my mind's fear. What I now feel is so free, so flowing, so completely empty of my judgment. It's so much easier to forgive myself through this love I'm feeling."

"I'm home," we heard Ethan call.

"We're in the sunroom. Let's have the bagels here. Do you want some help getting the plates out?" Iris asked.

Ethan came into the sunroom. His relaxed demeanor stunned me. The tension he had worn on his face and in his eyes for so long was mellowing into a soft glow. He was already embracing change. He said no help was needed, and soon returned, plates in hand.

Iris asked if I would share my garden dream with him. Ethan's tense, analytical gaze was quiet as I spoke. I took a break to eat, but I really needed that break to adjust to the space he was listening through. It was a space free of his usual intellectual appraisals. I never felt judgment from him, but during the past two or three years his intensity could sometimes feel self-righteous, closing off what my words wanted to communicate. I now understood his rigidness; Ethan's spirited imagination had gone astray as he served his own agendas. I wanted to tell him how much I appreciated all he did over the years, but the words did not need to be spoken. Both he and Iris had received my gratitude through the space we communicated within.

We were quiet as we ate, enjoying the mellowness we shared.

"I've studied music for years, learning everything I could possibly know about sound," Ethan said after some time. "But now I know how little I've learned. Micaela's words about pure sound originating from dimensions that aren't of the human heart and mind completely resonate with your soul's message. But only now, can I acknowledge the depth of wisdom it carries. My logic continues to warn me of believing nonsense, but I now know it fears a wisdom it can't create. It can only allow this wisdom. Fear is my mind's objection, but it's a powerful objection to dissolve."

"I feel much the same about my mind's self-judgment because it fuels doubt," Iris offered. "I sense the angel calling me to fill my mind and body with the vibrations of the rainbow and to share my expanding purity with it."

"I think you're right. Antonio's carving to me this year was a miniature statue of the angel, exactly as it is in the garden. It's much smaller, but it holds the energy the larger angel once did." Both Iris and Ethan nodded slightly. We knew all was in transformation, even the angel.

As I finished breakfast, I said I wanted to head back to the city. I would not return for at least a couple of weeks, as there were scheduled weekend events the orchestra was to perform in.

Iris asked that I let them know as soon as I heard from Micaela. She suggested she come to the house if she wanted to. She knew Antonio loved cooking for her. I nodded and was off.

It would be Thanksgiving weekend before I visited again. I had returned to my usual living and school environment, but how I lived within them was greatly changing. I bathed and polished Antonio's carvings as a sacred act of cleansing my own decay. Before washing each figure, I read its card while breathing into the energy of each word. I wanted to create space to touch my own sacred Self and hear its wisdom. I moved the table my carvings sat on to the bedroom. They would be the first thing my eyes visited when I awoke, and the last thing they visited before I fell asleep. I was practicing allowing the sacred essence of the first figure my eyes rested upon to be infused into my breath throughout the day, especially as I played my flute.

Situating the table under my window, I felt the magic of my time with Antonio while opening each carving in the garden. I understood that the sacred space I was "lifted" into when I was with Antonio and the angel, created the magic I felt. I recalled Antonio saying I would uncover the Mystery embedded in the carvings, and their words, when it was time to do so. Although I hadn't understood his words, I did not question him. They danced within wisdom's magical realm that was beyond doubt and questioning. In fact, through the space I was "lifted" into, magic was the only reality known.

"Interesting," I found myself reflecting aloud. "I

haven't neglected the carvings. Their sacred energies have been deeply planted within, gestating until I was ready to claim them as my own." Antonio knew exactly what he was doing, acting through a wisdom that only a master could embody. He created out of his spirit's passion that wanted only to extend its passion, needing no love, no acknowledgment, from others. He simply radiated the passionate, divine love he had realized within. Such an immense gift he was to all of us.

When I awoke this morning, my eyes fell upon the figure of a sacred woman petting a lion. Such tranquil peace they shared. Its card read, "Fear is giving power to the forceful roar of your own misunderstood shadow. Understanding sourced from nature's wisdom transmutes fear into love." It was becoming increasingly clear that Micaela was restating all Antonio had shared. What I had thought to be words of mythical characters unrelated to who I was, were the words of my very own soul Antonio had intuitively received.

It was late afternoon when my orchestra met for practice. It had been a difficult day, and early on, I lost any capacity to feel what I experienced in the quiet stillness of my bedroom. Mid-morning, I had met with the two members of my assigned orchestra trio. All trios were responsible for composing and playing a five-minute piece that was due in two weeks. Besides me, there was a female cello player and a male violin player. We all felt pressured because we needed to get much more accomplished to meet the deadline. As our frustrations reddened with anger, we decided to each compose a score that addressed our various concerns. We would meet in two days to play our separate pieces, then try to compose a score that pleased all. We retreated to our separate practice rooms where I attempted to breathe out my frustrations. But the pressure of time, and the accumulated irritation between us, consumed me. My breath remained rigidly tense. A half hour passed without focus, and I packed up to have lunch before my next class.

The end of the semester seemed to be stressing everyone, even my orchestra conductor. His cheerful, but demanding disposition was without its cheer this afternoon. Like him, I knew my sound was off-pitch and not in sync with the orchestra. He put his wand down to stop the music. "Dakari, your music is distracting me and others. Do you need some time alone to pull yourself together and play as you are able to play? Where is your passion to play as a master? Right now, you're disgracing any passion of a master."

The annoyance in his voice and eyes hit me in my gut, right where I needed to be hit. "You're correct. Please excuse me while I pull myself together. I offer no excuse, only my apology."

I went to the soundproof practice room. I sighed deeply, then sighed again and again, expanding my breath into each sigh, until I broke into sobs. "I'm insane to believe there's a divine presence to my Being that I can create music through. It's just my fanciful wish to be a truly great musician that's spurring my fallacy. How could I have been such a fool to believe this nonsense?" I yelled to the four walls that echoed back my desperation for relief. When the echo of my deep despair ended, all became quiet. I closed my eyes, opening space through my breath that had eluded me almost as soon as I left my apartment. Its welcomed calm invited me to feel its soothing presence. Slowly, gradually, the turbulence of my breath stilled. I began to play a simple, fun tune I loved as a third grader. It sang the beat and tones of different animals as we had imagined their traits such as playful, quick, strong, etc. Then we became each animal while the teacher played our recorded music.

Recalling the carving of the woman petting the lion, I imagined my body as a lion's body, feeling my strong, agile pace as I stalked my prey. My breath, and the notes of my flute, became the movement of my paws, cautiously inching toward my prey. I knew the slightest distraction, such as fear, would tease my death in the kill. My notes sounded the concentrated, centered focus of my stalk. Acutely attuning to the weaker pulse of my designated prey, my notes became that pulse. Completely focused within my still center, I waited for the exact moment of distraction in my prey to attack. It came, and I sprinted, my racing pulse completely attuned to the vibrations my prey emitted. Feeling its fear, I emitted every ounce of my powerful strength to freeze its fear in place. The purity of my flute's pulsating notes echoed off the wall, and I stopped playing to absorb their echo. I understood the lion's nature; the kill was the moment when the lion was the master. Fully attuned to nature's wisdom, it imagined the success of its kill, then acted on it through its still center. "Imagining sacred sound through my breath *is* real, and I don't want to freeze myself in fear any longer. I'm going back to play as a master."

The orchestra was just beginning a new piece, and my return was unnoticed. I sat, breathing every ounce of my still center deep within my being while imagining my breath's sacred sound flowing through my flute. Setting my flute's open mouth below my mouth, I breathed clarity through it as I had never done before . . . and the notes on my score came alive in light. They danced from the paper and into my fingers that floated over my flute's keyholes without effort. They danced through my breath and out of my flute into the conductor's wand, transforming it into a beam of light. Sparks flew from the wand's flame, blanketing the musicians with glimmering fireflies. Each instrument sang notes of joy, unifying as one song in a space that knew no resistance, no effort. I was "lifted" from my body, breathing sacredness to express sacredness.

At some point, the music stopped, and we sat in silence. We sensed we had shared a moment of magical synchronicity without knowing how or why. Opening my eyes, I saw my conductor dripping in sweat, breathing heavily and deeply, eyes still closed. After a couple of minutes, his eyes slowly opened, glimmering with sparks of fireflies. His voice broke the silence. "Dakari, I'm pleased to welcome you back as a budding musician of true mastery."

Someone commented we played beyond the time class should have ended. People began to pack their things up, needing to get to their next class. But I took my time, touching every keyhole to feel the breath I had lost myself to. "Sacred breath," I thought. "This is the breath I must always play through."

When my trio met two days later, I was the only one with a written score. "We decided we wanted to work with whatever score you created," they said, although a couple of suggestions were added. We liked our final score and looked forward to playing it for the others.

∾

ELEVEN

I had received an email from Micaela about a week after her visit. She suggested setting up a meeting over the internet, as it was a busy time. All agreed, and a meeting the week after Thanksgiving was confirmed. We always went to Ethan's parents for Thanksgiving dinner. They had a full-time cook who prepared a large meal for the many guests they invited. Their intense, rigid demeanor when at our home did not readily invite laughter. But when they had guests, they put on an entertaining show. They filled space with stories that created laughter while encouraging others to share their own jovial tales. It was easy to find space from the pretentious noise.

Iris' parents, Shaun, and Margaret, lived in Iowa and always came a day or two after Christmas for a week. They were art teachers in public schools. Their colorful, warm

Irish presence was much easier to be with than the loud posturing of Darren and Florence. I enjoyed sharing the Christmas decorations at Rockefeller Center with them every year. They looked for magic in the lights, seeking inspiration for their artwork and jointly crafted their yearly greeting cards that reflected the magic seized. Iris' younger brother and sister both had children, and it was easier for her to visit them a couple of times each year than for them to come here. I used to go with her in the summer, but as I got older, Iris accepted my wish not to go. On occasion, Ethan went with her.

I arrived home for Thanksgiving late Wednesday night. Everyone was tired and went to bed after a light conversation. I continued to feel a softness in Ethan that altered how he listened. The beauty he had reawakened to was like a gentle rain soaking into his being. Its soothing presence brought into balance a passion that had burned out-of-control and died. Like Earth during winter, the rain's tender droplets were nurturing and shaping the passionate, newly seeded life within him. The day after Thanksgiving, he asked me to follow him to his studio. His violin, usually off to the side, rested on a special stand next to the chair he sat on to compose music. His usual tools to create synthetic music now occupied the vacated space of his violin. He gestured for me to sit.

"I decided not to take new clients for a while, even though I'm losing two after the holiday season. I have more than I need and want to spend time developing my violin music. I play it a couple of hours each day. I've listened repeatedly to Micaela's ballad, losing myself to the purity of the notes my violin, and her voice, sang. When I turn the recorder off, I feel each fiber of my violin while attentive to the subtle vibrations it wishes to express through me. The more I lose my desire to control the music, the more receptive I feel to its vibrations. There have been brief moments when I felt meshed with my violin as its vibrations of purity reached into my cells to be expressed through me. Those moments are when my music expresses pure inspiration. I'm just now beginning to write notes that may lead to a full musical score one day.

"It's odd to be without a timeline to complete a project, and even more odd not to control the music's becoming with my analytical mind. I feel the extreme anxiety of my mind as it's being released from its role to control how the music is created. It can be difficult to get space from it and not force control over its agitations. When I can't feel inner peace, I stop what I'm doing, turn the recorder on, and breathe in the purity of Micaela's music. Its inspiration does embody the hope for creativity to thrive on this planet. I was quite naïve, always hoping to create the beauty of the music I knew at your birth without the necessary growth to do so. I'm grateful you listened to your own intuition and didn't get trapped into my music. I now recognize the wisdom that flowed through your entire life, even those years when your spirit was less present to you. You never were completely disconnected from it."

I smiled slightly, then shared my experience with my orchestra trio and conductor. Ethan's quiet presence remained absent of his analytical intensity. Like myself, he was finding the courage to act on his commitment to change.

"You're way ahead of me, and I applaud your musical magnificence. You're becoming an inspiration to all."

Noticing the recorder next to his stand, I asked him to play Micaela's ballad. As I listened, the white flame again appeared, pulsating with potential for new life, then dissolving into the radiant darkness. Merging the rhythm of my breath with the sensation the darkness radiated, wisdom's vibrations weaved themselves into my being as soft whispers. "The sacred hum you sense is the vibration of the multidimensional layers of the cosmic mind that is your mind, too. Breathe its creative intelligence into your Beingness. Perceive and create within a lifted, expanded sense of beauty."

When Ethan turned the recorder off a few minutes after the ballad ended, he said it was dinnertime, and Iris could probably use some help. Antonio was not working over the holiday weekend. When we got to the house, Iris said she ordered dinner that should be delivered in about 15 minutes. Her warm nature glowed with renewed vitality. While waiting, Iris talked about research related to the goddess Iris she began a couple of weeks ago. After meeting Micaela, she recalled an image of the goddess that Margaret, her mother, had painted for her bedroom when she was young and called to see what she knew about her.

"Mom said the goddess Iris is a messenger of the gods. She uses a rainbow as a bridge to carry messages of peace between Heaven and Earth." She and Ethan still referred to their parents in the traditional manner. "In some mythologies, the rainbow is believed to be the flowing, multicolored robe of Iris, and the rainbow-colored flowers to be a continuation of her robe on Earth. The iris color defines the message of the gods. But I couldn't accept her explanation because it separated Heaven from Earth, and gods from humans. After more searching, I found the rainbow body described as the final stage of being before enlightenment because the body has integrated all energies of the cosmic mind. I understood why the angel told me to fill my body with the vibrations of the rainbow.

"Recently, I washed the angel when Antonio wasn't here. As I began, your dream about the musical vibrations the irises sang, and how they lost their form to create a rainbow, became vivid in my imagination. I even sensed sounds, although faintly. Earth's opened void became present, as well as my fear of it. Placing my hands on the angel's open palms, a situation from my past, charged with guilt and shame, arose. I gasped in shock at my actions, and my mind filled with harsh comments. I sobbed from my pain. As my tears flowed onto the angel's eyes, I cleansed its face, and I imagined my cells cleansed of guilt and shame. After attaching the angel to its pedestal, I tenderly washed the serpents on it, offering them my judgment of this memory and others. Washing the flame, a fiery passion moved through my breath, nudging me to burn anything that suffocated love. The pure passion I felt helps me to better relate to the passion Ethan felt at your birth."

My own experiences with the flame made it easy to relate to the passion Iris spoke of, and I shared some of my experience with it. "Since the first time I heard Micaela play, the image of the angel's flame has appeared. Its radiance pierces my insides as if to look for space to exist within me." I went on to share how the flame dissipates into the blackness of a vortex whirlpool it emerged from, and how this blackness pulsates with a wisdom full of loving passion. I also shared what I had just experienced while listening to Micaela's ballad. Ethan had just begun to talk when the doorbell rang. Dinner had arrived.

"Pick a good bottle of wine," Ethan called to Iris as he headed to the door. "We all need to relax and enjoy the meal."

"It feels a bit odd experiencing Ethan so tranquil," I said through my own lightness.

Iris agreed. We were all beginning to know and share ourselves in a very new and different way. It was the dawning of a whole new life. While we were quite clueless about what would manifest, we were ready to release what we knew no longer served us. We also recognized that sacrifices accompanied change and were already experiencing some of the challenges that deep change evoked. But while wary of what laid ahead, we all knew it was better to face those challenges, than to suffocate within the stagnant energies of decay.

The end-of-semester pressure that was universally shared continued to infuse itself through the air while threatening to erupt tightening nerves. But the feverish pace made the week pass quickly. It was Saturday morning, and I was at my apartment, as my orchestra was to perform at an event that evening. Our meeting with Micaela would be in the early afternoon, and I was feeling apprehensive about it. When I spoke with Iris and Ethan last night, they were curious as to why we were together. They sensed more was involved than our experiences as a family. I told them the angel had said we had important work to do, and our family bonds were not of primary importance to this work.

"I'm not surprised you're asking about this," Micaela said after Iris jumped right in with questions. "You're correct, being together is not a coincidence. Your souls chose to be together on Earth at this time prior to your birth. You and Ethan have had some karma needing resolution, but your karma is not as heavy as in most people, and some has already been resolved through your inner work. I'll address your karma shortly, Dakari.

"Your souls are together to help root crystalline light into Earth's soil. It's the light of the divine heart and mind, a Pure Awareness, unaffected by creation's dual forces of positive, male energy and negative, female energy. Your shared trauma at Dakari's birth catapulted your awareness into this sacred space of divine love and passion. It's a space where the creative passion of the sacred Masculine, and the compassionate understanding of the sacred Feminine, exist in complete balance. These energies have always existed deep within each of you, but for most of your adult lives, they've been out of balance. And this imbalance between positive and negative forces within you has created the confusion you now know: what is right or wrong, good, or bad, and on and on. There's constant tension about which opposite is best to act upon, and often, self-judgment of the choices made. These energies are your demons, and they live as parasites in your cells while feeding off your life force.

"Who you have believed yourself to be is not your truth. It's merely a persona, a fragment of your being whose energies need resolution. Spirit's pure wisdom needs no resolution. It's free of creation's opposing forces and the fear and tension that accompany these dual forces. Out of the deepest compassion to resolve your suffering, the sacred Feminine slowly reveals your demons to embrace through Her love. The force of your hardened energies is dissolved through this love, freeing your mind of its fear and tension. You come to exist within a depthless space of free-flowing grace that wants only to share its radiance through you.

"Iris, you felt this profound love at Dakari's birth, and you embraced the fear of your dark womb through a light unknown to your adult mind. Your allowance of this light helped to bind Dakari's earthly awareness with the love of his soul, and not with the fear of your mind. It also inspired you to find the strength to return to your body and raise him. Ethan, you also felt passionate light, and your allowance of this light supported Iris. It also extended your Beingness, enabling your experience of the crystalline clarity that is of divine imagination. Its profound, sensual love softened your mind's habit to scrutinize sound, which would have greatly dimmed the clarity you knew. Holding Dakari as a newborn, your shared light 'lifted' the awareness of both of you into a state of exalted grace. This sublime light strengthened the bond between the love of Dakari's soul and his human mind and body. You already know it was the heavy, unresolved emotions remaining in both of you that pulled your awareness back into density as time passed."

"Were the difficulties I experienced at Dakari's birth inevitable?"

"Intuitively, you knew you could not birth Dakari in your state of fear, although you were not consciously aware of this knowing. But you were acutely aware that your fear was doing harm and tried to release it through the tactics of your mind. When you finally surrendered your mind's control out of complete desperation for your lives, your awareness was lifted from your body, enabling your near-death experience of light. The potential existed for both of you to die, but you found the courage to birth Dakari through light and reenter your body. You have much strength that is yet to be acknowledged."

"The pattern I was stuck in was growing increasingly unbearable," Iris said through a voice that reflected her pain. "I understand much better why both of us got stuck."

"You hear my words with clarity only because of everything you've experienced as you tried to change your human self. You now know the futility of your mind's efforts to bring you lasting peace. You can understand the need to work with your mind's fears through a sacredness that won't engage in its endless battles. Slowly, gradually, your carbon-based body that has trapped you in duality will be transmuted into a crystalline-based body that will allow the integration of your divine Self."

Micaela shifted her attention to me, sharing the fullness of her presence through her shimmering, green eyes. It was as if her light was not contained within the computer. "Dakari, you are a master of divine love and wisdom. There was a small degree of ancestral karma in the biological body you inherited at birth, but the light present at your birth, and the abundant, loving guidance you were raised with, have resolved most of this karma. The karma served you well because it gave you an understanding of what fear is and how it blocks your creative passion. Your current willingness to embrace your sacred Self as a part of your Beingness is creating some anxiety in your mind. Acknowledge its doubt through love. In time, your mind will see how your soul serves it without need to control or eliminate it. It will adapt and learn how to create in partnership with your sacred Self. Claim the truth of your Beingness. Be the master you know yourself to be."

Micaela's eyes remained fixed on mine for a few moments as if to pierce through any doubt, then she looked away. While I was stunned to hear her words, I was also relieved. They gave me permission to claim this more passionate presence of my own Beingness. Tears fell from Iris' eyes, and Ethan shared a soft, loving smile.

All was quiet for a short time. When Micaela suggested we end the night, all agreed. She said to contact her through email if we wanted to meet again. I filled the tub with hot water and essential oils. It would be a long night with the orchestra, and I needed to prepare myself for it.

TWELVE

Somehow, I managed to get through the end-of-semester crunch. I arrived in Westchester three days before Christmas, and the yearly challenge of finding the perfect gift for Iris and Ethan was upon me. Normally, I would be racing about in my usual Christmas shopping frenzy. But on the train, I decided this year would be different. I wanted my gifts to express a deeper meaning to the peace Christmas was meant to represent. But what gifts could express this peace? I would have loved Antonio's advice, but he was on vacation for a couple of weeks. He had been busy preparing a major fundraising dinner that Iris and Ethan put on each year for the theater group, and his break was well-earned. He would probably tell me to listen to my own heart, even if I could ask him.

When I got to the house, I found a note that they were attending a holiday event and would be home late. I poured a glass of wine, went into the sunroom, put on some music, and turned on the tiffany lamp that occupied the marble table overlooking the slumbering garden. Dusk was on the horizon. The window faced east, so I could not see the sunset, but its colors reflected off the blanket of snow covering the sleeping ground. The snow's icy crystals created sparkles of colorful light. A sense of awe at the Earth's beauty, and the profound peace this beauty lovingly radiated, arose. "The Earth's beauty is my beauty," I found myself saying aloud to Antonio's carvings on the table. "Peace exists: I merely need to disengage from my inner chatter to Be that peace."

I breathed deeply, opening to the expansiveness of the beauty I was feeling. A dove that Antonio had carved in ivory reflected the colors of the tiffany lamp upon its body. I delicately placed it in my palm, acknowledging its beauty as my beauty. Antonio had given Ethan and Iris this dove when I left for college, telling them the dove was recognized as a spirit messenger, a liaison, between the soul's intuitive sense and the mind's logical knowing. He wrote on its card, "Peace: Completeness, Wholeness, Harmony. Look within, not without." Iris said the dove's simple, yet elegant design helped her understand that my departure was not a loss. It was an opportunity to embrace a new stage of life, one that offered an opportunity to empty her outer and inner space of unnecessary distractions.

I recalled Micaela's words to her and Ethan about looking for completeness outside of themselves rather than inside. When they read Antonio's words four years ago, neither of them could understand their deeper meaning. They had relied on their minds for understanding, which was creating the thick, brick wall between their established patterns of thought and freedom from them. Yet, how they understood and acted on the words then, also opened the door for a deeper understanding now. "Nothing is right or wrong," I realized. "Reality is a matter of how complete we are from within. The more we free ourselves from the force of cluttered thoughts, the more life's beauty is seen. Amazing, we create and recreate our reality with every breath taken. It wasn't only me that called Micaela to the music café; the deep desire of Iris and Ethan to break through what they felt so stuck in, also called her there."

Returning the dove to the table, it again reflected the rainbow colors on its ivory body. An image of Iris, wrapped in a shawl with the rainbow colors, appeared. "A rainbow-colored cashmere shawl would be a great gift. Tomorrow, I'll investigate places that make custom shawls." Nothing came to me for Ethan. He had the means to buy whatever he needed, although he was never wasteful with money. "Just relax. Something will show itself tomorrow as I shop," I reassured myself.

The semester had been grueling, and with only one semester left, it was a strange feeling to finally be looking at the end of my time as a student. But I never wanted to leave learning behind. I assumed it was a matter of creating what learning would become. I had applied to the Vermont Symphony Orchestra a month ago and was waiting for their response. My orchestra conductor shared that after he sent his reference, my creativity had bloomed into a true level of mastery, and he sent an updated letter to them. I knew I had a very good chance of getting an interview. I just needed my nerves to remain settled to avoid their interference with the clarity of sound I wanted to breathe through my instruments at my audition.

I was tired and hungry and wanted something to eat before going to bed. As I stood to go to the kitchen, the soft-glowing solar lights around the angel called my attention. Iris never put lights on the angel, saying it radiated its own light, but the solar lights around it accentuated the Christmas vine that flowed from its open palms, over its gown. A small tree by the angel, decorated with multicolored lights, replaced the colors of her rainbow garden. Taking a walk into the winter garden, I felt a still, quiet strength emanating from the angel. The white cedar vine flowing from its open palms released an aroma of purity into the air. The fresh baby breath placed in its crown this morning appeared untouched by the cold. When our eyes met, I felt stillness emanating from them. "Do not seek peace. Be still. Hear the quiet voice of your sacred Self speaking through love, and Be peace," its eyes said to my heart.

I awoke before dawn, the house completely still. But my mind erupted into the stillness, stirring noisy chatter about what needed to be done. I breathed deeply, stilling its thoughts. "The perfect gift will show itself if I stay aware in trust and not succumb to tension," I thought. I was too tired to eat dinner last night and was hungry. A coffee shop in town served great food and coffee, and I would decide things from there. A sunny, crisp winter day greeted me after a relaxed shower. A light snow had fallen three days ago. Reflecting the sun's light, I was reminded that I am so much more than just my physical mind and body.

When I arrived at the coffee shop, a girl I knew from high school came with a menu. It was early for most shoppers, so we had time for a small chat. She was an art student, and I asked if she knew where I could get a custom-made cashmere shawl. She directed me to a farm that had opened a few years ago. It was owned and managed by Tibetan monks who raised their own goats for the cashmere. They treated the animals well, and their products were high-quality. She described the farm as a special place to visit, although it was over two hours away, further north. She also said one of the monks was an artist and sold his paintings. She loved his work and had bought one of his pieces. I got the address and texted a note to Ethan that I wouldn't be home until early evening.

I had never heard of this place and googled information while eating. The pictures, taken in late spring or early summer, showed the farm in a rich, green valley that was nestled within a wooded, hilly area surrounding it. It was evident the animals were treated well. The five oil paintings shown were landscapes of Tibet and of the farm. I felt the peace they exuded. "I know I'll find the right gifts here."

I was on my way, driving the backroads for most of the drive. I was gifted a small car when I graduated high school but did not get out for long drives often. I seldom took it to the city, as using Mass Transit was much easier. So, when I did take long drives, I really enjoyed them, especially when exploring a new place and in no hurry to get there. It was a time to fully appreciate a new landscape, one that was gestating seeds of future magnificence. The town the farm was in had many restored, old homes with oak trees lining the streets. The buildings stood tall, seeming to share their pride in the quality of artisanship they embodied. I parked the car to admire the buildings and stretch my legs with a short walk. "Look at us," they whispered through the winds that touched their surface. "Our grandeur is the caring love and attention of the craftsmen who labored to bring us into existence." I acknowledged the beauty they offered to those with eyes to see it.

The farm was not far from the center of town, and I almost missed its unassuming entry sign. There were a handful of beautifully built barns with solar roofs for heating. I understood these panels provided heat for animals whose hair had been shaved to prevent shock from the cold. These monks knew exactly what they were doing, practicing humanity in their ways. While the barns were open to visitors, the animals occupied a roped off area away from human touch. Signs asked that sudden, loud noise be avoided and to not feed or touch the animals unless supervised. There were five barns with about 20 goats in each barn. Two of the barns were colder because none of the goats had been shaved. The other three barns with shaved goats were warmer, but coats were needed. Even the goats had coverings on them. Their contentment was noticeable.

A small, middle-aged monk was supervising children as they petted the goats. His warm eyes caught mine, inviting me to do the same. I sensed the goat trusting the monk as he gently told it another visitor wished to touch it. It did not resist my touch. The children left, and he asked if there was anything special that I was looking for. I told him about the rainbow shawl, but also asked if art pieces were available. He said there were, but I would have to see Brother Tom to view them. I was directed to a small cottage close to the barns.

A sign on the door said to knock, enter, and have a seat. Brother Tom would assist shortly. It was a small room with a handful of wooden chairs. A catalogue with about 10 paintings was available. It said some paintings may have already been sold, but others not in the catalogue were also available. The mountains of Tibet were stunning. In one painting, an ominous cloud hovered over a jagged peak with snow lifting into the air from its barren sides. I sensed the power of Zeus breathing through the winds that pulverized its peak. Its energy was markedly different from the energy of this farm's landscape in mid-fall when the leaves peaked into the fullness of their fall colors. There appeared to be a mild wind whistling through the trees, assisting with the release of dead leaves from their limbs. I breathed deeply, feeling the vibrations the colors sang. They captured the song that lived within me. "This monk is attuned to and grounded within his new land, just as he was in his homeland," I thought. "He is of nature, regardless of the specific place he lives in."

About 10 minutes later, a young couple and a monk who I assumed was Brother Tom entered the waiting room. He was assuring them their painting would be shipped right away. His small, thin frame wore a paint-splattered apron over jeans and a T-shirt. He was an older man whose shimmering, brown eyes occupied his entire face. His long beard was also splattered with paint. After the couple left, he said he needed about five minutes with a warm smile. A young, slim, Asian man in loose-fitting pants and a heavy, cashmere shawl and hat, entered. He stood quietly by the door without making eye contact. I assumed he was a monk.

When Brother Tom returned, he handed a large box with a postal address to the monk while speaking his mother-tongue. He introduced himself with a slight bow, his hands folded into a prayer. I nodded my head slightly while folding my hands as he had done. "This time of year, I love," he said through a soft, gentle voice while sitting opposite me. His English was correct, although spoken remarkably slow and with a slight accent. "Many people to share my work with. A great honor to have others appreciate the love and attention I give my paintings. Is there anything that interests you?"

"I sensed the care you give your paintings. They're unique and quite beautiful. I also sensed your deep connection to nature. I don't know exactly what I'm looking for. I was thinking of buying a rainbow shawl for Iris, my mother, but wanted to look at your artwork as well."

"Are you an artist?"

I smiled at his question, wondering if I could call myself an artist. "I'd like to consider myself an artist, but I suppose I'm evolving into one. I play the flute and piccolo and hope to get a job with a professional orchestra when I graduate from college this spring."

The light in his eyes pierced through my eyes as if wishing to touch my spirit, the real artist within me. "Your name?"

"Dakari."

"Dakari, I believe you will be a master of music. I see it budding in your eyes."

He led me into his studio. Light, streaming in from a picture window with a southern exposure, filled the room. Oil paintings from his catalogue hung on its white walls. Now directly exposed to the life force each painting pulsated, I felt drawn into their secrets of nature. While looking at each painting, I breathed deeply to receive the wisdom each embodied. Before seeing all of them, Brother Tom called my attention to him. On a small side wall that had been empty, another piece now hung.

"I created this painting three years ago, but until you came, I did not know who it was for. I believe it is for Iris. I titled it, *Imagination: Passion Meeting Love*, but Iris can give it any name she likes."

I barely registered his words as I was pulled into the passionate love the painting radiated. There was a black, oval-shaped egg, almost the width of a circle that radiated the compassionate waters of my visions. On its outer rim was a refined cloud of light with specks of light throughout, which I sensed to be stardust. Just breaking through the black egg, on its right side, was a translucent, white stallion. Embodying the wild, undomesticated brilliance of its spirit, its bodily form was loosely defined, and its gray eyes were ablaze with light. Poised in the stance of a full gallop, the stallion emitted active strength. At the point where the stallion intersected the dark egg, a rainbow exploded its life force outward, filling space around the egg with the subtle vibrations of its colors. A light, almost transparent gray, filled space about the stallion, and I recalled the gray center of the angel's flame.

"Ah, the gray center of my flame represents the two charged forces of creation that the sacred Masculine and Feminine hold in balance," I said half aloud, recognizing the depth of this work. "Passion meeting love, free of fear's resistance. This painting is not only for Iris; it's also for Ethan, my father."

"You recognize a sacred essence in the painting. There are many ways to understand it because creation's deepest Mystery can never be fully known. Its creative life force forever expands through souls who unite with its passion. I trusted a person who honored life's Mystery would own this. In receiving the energy this painting holds, one is guided to breathe more deeply into the sacred depths of life's Mystery and carry its inspiration forward into the world."

"Iris and Ethan are just breaking into the tip of that iceberg and will benefit greatly from it."

We settled the finances, although it felt awkward to exchange money for it. I knew exactly how Iris felt when she paid Antonio for the angel. Its value could not be defined through money. I also purchased gift certificates for the in-laws on both sides of the family. I knew Ethan and Iris would love to meet Brother Tom and driving Iris' parents here during their visit would be the perfect opportunity to do so. Darren and Florence would be leaving a couple of days after Christmas. They lived in different tropical areas during the coldest winter months. It would be a while before they would get here. They enjoyed visiting a large lake in a nearby tourist area every summer. Most likely, they would stop at the farm during their summer travels.

As Brother Tom was boxing the painting, I shared that Iris and Ethan would love to meet him, and one gift certificate was for Iris' parents who would be visiting after Christmas. He said he looked forward to it, then suggested I stop at the shop where cashmere items were available. They were also works of art. He pointed me in the direction of the shop as he handed me my painting. After placing it in my car, I headed there. It was barn shaped with windows and solar panels on the roof. Sun and soft music filled an uncluttered, rustic space. The items, artfully arranged throughout, gave the space the appearance of an art studio. It was busy, yet amazingly peaceful. Scarves with designs woven through them caught my attention. Soon a monk, about the age of Brother Tom, was at my side. He was dressed in a light sweater and loose-fitting pants.

"Can I help you?" he asked through still, peaceful eyes and a voice even more slow and accented than

Brother Tom's.

I was holding a red scarf with the symbol of the Bodhi Tree on one end of it. I knew this tree was often recognized as a symbol of hope, and the red color emitted the pure passion of spirit. "The red dye is intensely vibrant, but the softness of the cashmere fiber tempers it. The earthy brown of the Bodhi design is a softened passion. It's beautiful."

"You give attention to the sacred. Few do," the monk said, his eyes glimmering with delight.

My eye caught a light-blue shawl with a white lotus on it, and the angel's feet came to mind. The monk began to comment on the lotus. "The beauty of the lotus rises out of the thick mud of its roots. It reminds me that I must rise above the dense mud of pain and suffering to know beauty. It's never easy to go deep into the mud to know what hides within it. But when we do, we befriend what once caused us so much anguish. Grace is always present to help us if we allow its holy presence. There is no virtue in suffering and there is a way out of it. Even Buddha came to understand that allowing love was far more powerful than allowing self-punishment."

"I understand your words and appreciate the love you put into your work. These are perfect gifts for people who can also appreciate the fullness of what they offer. I'm glad I found my way to this farm." He acknowledged my words with a nod as I paid him.

∽o

THIRTEEN

I arrived at the house an hour or so after dusk. The Christmas lights caught my attention, and I wanted to take a closer look at them after putting my car in the garage. The moon was waning from its fullness a week ago, but it still offered much light on this clear night. Its light, and the light of the endless stars, lit my path to the front of the house. I looked for a stallion among them, blazing its brilliant passion within the radiant darkness of the sky's cosmic sea. Two hollowed-out deer holding the darkness of the night were illuminated with the white lights of their frames. A large pine tree in the house, dressed in multicolored lights, reflected its colors on the snow before the deer, honoring them. "The dark womb of life's Mystery within, and the shimmering light of spirit, expressing their explosive union through the multicolored lights of the rainbow," I mused aloud.

I found Iris and Ethan in the sunroom, wrapping paper covering the floor. Tomorrow was Christmas Eve, and they were busy. We always had a buffet dinner for this occasion, shared with a handful of different guests each year who could use company. It was a relaxed dinner, free of gift exchange other than special foods and drinks that everyone contributed to the buffet. We never knew what would create our holiday bounty, enjoying the element of surprise. The hodgepodge of food and drink, and the informal, relaxed atmosphere always made this night special. Christmas dinner, hosted by Darren and Florence at their home, was not an event I looked forward to. "Interesting," I thought, "maybe my mind doesn't enjoy this time, but for my soul, it's another experience to be sensuously embraced, free of drama. Beloved mind, why not embrace the adventure of Christmas dinner with those who challenge your comfort level?"

"Hi Dakari," Ethan said. "Welcome back."

Iris gave me a small hug, wishing me a Merry Christmas. "We still have lots of gifts to wrap. Sandwiches and salad are in the kitchen. Help yourself when you're hungry."

"Sounds good. I've got lots to wrap myself. Will take dinner to my room to get things done."

The day of Christmas Eve was much the same. Everyone was busy with last-minute details. I had the regular job of going to specialty shops in town to buy various foods and wines as Iris and Ethan occupied the kitchen with cooking. I enjoyed this time, tasting interesting foods at gourmet shops and sharing Christmas cheer. An unusual atmosphere of genuine warmth filled the air, and I embraced this warmth.

The smells of Christmas candles, and foods being prepared when I returned, danced through the air while inviting my senses to open and receive the rich depths of their origins as never before. Five guests came that evening, ranging from 25 to 73 years of age, none of whom were from the same family. One was not Christian, but she enjoyed celebrating the peace the holiday represented. All brought specialties of their different ethnic backgrounds. The buffet made for a lively discussion of the many traditions each culture shared with food and drink. A perfect evening in many ways.

I was up early Christmas morning and went for a walk. Christmas lights were lit, celebrating the day. I imagined kids waking up to their uncontainable excitement. "Our ability to embrace life's magic gets buried beneath the adult mind of fear and its apprehension," I thought. I recalled the time when rumors reached my ear as a kindergartner about the fallacy of Santa Claus. I asked Iris if it's true Santa Claus was not real. She said the spirit of Santa is very real, and that his spirit lives through any person willing to imagine being him. I appreciated her uncommitted, but sensitive response this Christmas more than ever.

When I returned, the coffee had just finished brewing. We put a tray of food together and headed to the living room to share gifts. As soon as we sat, Ethan handed me a gift. "We've had this for over a month now, and each day it's gotten more difficult to wait to give it to you," he said affectionately.

It was a solid sterling piccolo with 14K gold added to its tenon, the piece that joined the mouthpiece, or head-joint, with its body. I held it in my left palm, feeling every keyhole with my free hand. I closed my eyes, imagining the sound I wanted my piccolo to resonate. "The passionate, loving union of the golden sun and silver moon bursting forth as sensuous splendor," I murmured half aloud as I placed it under my mouth. A joyful tune, unknown to me, freely flowed through its silver and gold body. When I finished the song and returned it to its case, I beamed with pure pleasure.

I handed the painting to Iris while telling Ethan it was for him, too. He moved to sit beside Iris as she opened it. I watched their eyes brighten with joy when they first saw it, then silently explore its features. Ethan's intense gaze softened, and his face relaxed. Iris moved her hand above the stallion, then the black egg, and finally the rainbow. "The stallion feels intensely alive with creativity, so intense it could burn itself to ashes. The black egg radiates a soothing love that's beckoning the stallion's burning intensity to be received by it. I feel this black egg as I felt my womb when I carried you. It was passionately alive with creativity as the rawness of new life was weaved into your body's form. The explosive joy I sense in the rainbow is the joy I knew when I received you as a newly born child. You were the rainbow as a creation of immense, passionate love."

Finding the card with its title, Ethan read it aloud, "*Imagination: Passion Meeting Love.* So very fitting," he murmured. "This painting is beautifully crafted. It's breathtaking. Who's the artist?"

I told them about Brother Tom and how long the painting sat. I also shared his belief that the person who would own the painting could acknowledge the Mystery his painting embodied. Perhaps that person would even pierce through life's Mystery and know it as the infinite depths of their Beingness. When I mentioned the gift card for Iris' parents and that Brother Tom knew we would be coming very soon, they were pleased.

They handed me a photo album. None of us took many photos, and we had only a couple of them. They said when they looked at the photos, many of them were with the angel.

"I always knew the angel was a part of you," Iris said, "and that you belonged more to it, than you did to us."

"While putting the album together, we recalled the angel's words that our memories as a family were not of primary importance to our purpose of being together.

Its words helped us to accept what Iris and I have always felt, but could never acknowledge to each other," Ethan added. "I suppose we just weren't ready to do so. Making this album helped bring completion to our time together."

"I suppose the gate to a life that doesn't bind us through our shared biology was opened at my birth, and we had to accept that opening to walk through the gate. I've never felt either of you block any part of my life, and I thank you for the freedom you've always given me. Your courage on your own inner journeys, and the gift of light at my birth, inspire me."

I handed them their cashmere gifts while sharing the monk's words about the lotus. "The shawl is perfect for the winter season when I'm outside putting flowers on the angel. It's odd how I've given little attention to the ivory lotuses of the angel's feet. I must finally be ready to peer into what really lies at the core of my dark roots and not shrink in despair from what I see. I have suffered from getting stuck in the muddy roots of a love that knew judgment. Perhaps I accepted my suffering as a necessary penance for my misdeeds."

Ethan appeared not to hear Iris. He was feeling his scarf, tracing his finger over the Bodhi Tree, eyes closed. At some point, he looked up and thanked me.

It was mid-afternoon when we arrived for dinner. Darren and Florence appeared more tired than usual. They were aging but refused to acknowledge this change, insisting on the same non-stop activities they had always known. Perhaps a slower pace threatened awareness of their inner tension. Lack of peace was their unacknowledged but nagging companion. They were far less animated than at Thanksgiving, but this change went unnoticed by the many guests who carried the excitement of the festive day. It was the first time Darren and Florence expressed gratitude when the last guest left, and we could relax in a space with a lot less noise and activity. Perhaps they would come to appreciate the quiet and explore what it had to offer as their stamina to handle what they once did, lessened.

When they opened the gift certificate, I shared an edited story about my time with Brother Tom and the farm. When they asked about the painting I bought, Iris began to describe it.

"Remember all the beautiful sunsets we've shared sitting on the deck as the light of the sun gave way to the light of the moon? We always acknowledged how beautiful this time of day was, and how its colors melded with the colors in my rainbow garden. In the painting, a white stallion emits the sun's blazing passion, and a black, oval egg radiates the moon's soothing love. The stallion knows that love is a part of it, too, and in the poise of a full gallop is breaking through the black egg to claim this love. A rainbow explodes outward from the point where passion and love unite." She shared the painting's title, suggesting that the power of our imagination is far greater than what we ever thought possible.

Iris did well. They were absorbed in her words, then expressed their desire to see the painting soon after they returned from their trip. Their gratitude for the gift card felt genuine, which I was unused to. We left soon afterward. While I enjoyed the holiday, I was grateful for the return of quiet, and that Christmas was a once-a-year event.

My musing was ended by Iris' voice. "While sharing the description of the painting, I understood, with greater clarity, that the dark *is* of light and the light *is* of dark. It's odd that love, the elixir that brings them into balance, is so difficult to embrace. I had lost all sense of the love my soul always wanted to share. No wonder we humans lack inspiration." She sighed, then added almost in a whisper, "The path of the rainbow is the path of faith I surrender my breath to."

Margaret and Shaun had mailed gifts that sat under the tree, along with their gifts from us. In the past, we all found ourselves by the tree ready to share them when the moment spontaneously struck. This year, I wanted the gifts opened soon after they arrived to plan a trip to the farm. It was odd how much I looked forward to visiting there again. I sensed something was there needing my attention that I failed to notice on my first visit. Perhaps, though, I was just looking forward to seeing Brother

Tom, as I was missing Antonio. "I'll rarely see him when I move," I thought with a bit of sadness. I understood why Antonio discouraged my dependency on him to touch sacred realms as I grew. I had to feel and trust the wisdom of my soul and spirit and find inner strength to move through my challenges. He wanted me to realize that he shared so much more than his physical presence and spoken words. What always captivated me was Antonio's sacred Self, and its radiance was not contained within, nor limited to, his physical body. It was a divine presence that souls communicated through, and I was just stepping onto the bridge that would enable me to grow in the intuitive ways of sacred communication.

They arrived early afternoon, the day after Christmas, and would be flying back on New Year's Day. It was an early flight, and they spent much of the afternoon resting from their hectic morning. But by dinnertime, the fatigue of the flight was a distant memory. Iris and Ethan took them for a long walk around the house and into the garden to see the lights, and they entered through the front where the tree lights were lit. I quickly brought the tray of cheese and fruit I had prepared into the living room. Placing it on the table in front of the tree, I invited everyone to enjoy the food.

Iris looked at me, grinning, then said, "Well, since we're all here with plenty to appease our appetites, how about we share our gifts now?"

The painting had been moved to a corner near the

tree area, hidden from view. When the gift certificate to the farm was opened, Ethan brought the painting into full view. As artists, Shaun and Margaret recognized the brilliance in the technique, and the endless possible meanings it offered. When Iris shared its title, they said they had never considered imagination to be the union of passion and love. Yet, they recognized how brilliantly the painting portrayed its title.

"The more I allow the painting to draw me into it, the more I recognize the simple, but elegant clarity it speaks," Margaret said. "When I think back on my paintings that shared beauty, they were the paintings I felt most passionate about. I didn't realize it then, but I had lost myself to what the painting wanted to express, leaving my analytical eye behind. If I had allowed judgment, I would've lost my connection to what the painting wanted to express."

Iris shared her understanding of the rainbow body. While Shaun and Margaret were more sensitive to artistry than most, neither had a mystical experience that would assist their knowing of the sacred energies the rainbow held. They asked if she would hang the painting so they could sit with it and soak in its inspiration, and it was hung in the sunroom. They were excited about seeing Brother Tom's paintings and choosing one for their own home.

The next day, I often saw Iris in the sunroom with

Margaret and Shaun talking more about the painting and carvings. They had seen the carvings before, but they were looking at their words with a new eye, asking questions about what they could represent that they failed to sense before. Ethan was busy with a client at another location, so I wandered into his studio to play my new piccolo. I listened to Micaela's ballad first, feeling the depth of loving passion she infused into her music. Her level of mastery could not be taught by techniques learned through the mind; she was free of any influences that could taint the purity of her music. When I finally put my piccolo to my mouth, I was aware only of what my heart wanted to sing.

As we drove to the farm the next day, the discussion between Iris and her folks continued, but my input was also asked for at times. "Dakari, before you play your flute, do you imagine how you want to play the notes?" Shaun asked.

"I do, but I don't imagine the specific notes themselves. I imagine my breath, full of light, carrying my spirit's inspiration through my flute. Expanding my breath deep within me where cluttered thoughts don't exist, I *feel* the sacredness of the sound I wish to play. I suppose you could call what I sense divine imagination, rather than mindful imagination. What I sense beyond my mind's imagination. My mind assists with the technical details of using the correct keyholes for the notes, but it's increasingly willing to step aside and allow the grace within to direct the flow of my breath through the flute. The resonance the notes sing is the real magic in music."

"I'm beginning to see the fallacy of what I've told my students about how to imagine," Shaun said after some time. "I wasn't guiding them to perceive through anything other than the minds they had become so dependent on. No wonder most of them had difficulty imagining artwork with deep, aesthetic beauty. In fact, with all the mental techniques I taught, I was encouraging them to remain in their cage of mental activity. It was a rare student who broke through the rigid black and white constraints of their minds, and I admit this breakthrough was due to that student's creativity, not to my suggestions. How differently I am starting to see things."

Margaret said they were increasingly pressured to teach statewide standards of art appreciation, and how those standards removed her students from the appreciation of aesthetic beauty the Arts were supposed to encourage. I realized how lucky I was to have had the education I did. I was glad when silence finally found its way into the car.

FOURTEEN

The farm was far less crowded than a week ago. It was the after Christmas low, giving us lots of time to look at the paintings. After knocking and walking in, we found the entry door into his art studio open. Brother Tom greeted us with his warm bow, then led us into his studio. "I don't have the Christmas crowds, so I allow people to come right in."

It was a cloudy day, but the paintings reflected their own light. They began looking at the ones I had already seen, and I ventured to those I had yet to see. Brother Tom remained with the others. A small painting of two lakes, nestled within the Himalayas, immediately caught my attention. I recognized them as Lake Manasarovar and Lake Rakshastal of the Tibetan Plateau, as I had learned of them in a class on mythology. Lake Rakshastal was a crescent-shaped, saltwater lake west of Lake Manasarovar that was connected to it by a natural, small water channel. It was known as a poisonous, demonic lake with undrinkable water and barren landscape. Fearing its evil powers, the gods avoided this lake. Lake Manasarovar was a much larger, freshwater lake with the circular shape of the sun. The gods believed it embodied purity and light, often bathing in it for its purifying powers. Humans had adopted the gods' beliefs, fearing, and avoiding Lake Rakshastal but extending great effort to visit Lake Manasarovar for its powers of purification. Tibetan monasteries existed along the mountain cliffs of Lake Manasarovar.

A vortex whirlpool was painted at the center of Lake Manasarovar. "It's the fierce howl of the mountain's undomesticated breath. I know the wind's raw passion that whips the water's surface into its opposing rotations to create the void at its center. I've also felt the water embrace the wind's passionate stirring as it surrendered, without resistance, into the unknown of the suctioning chasm the winds stirred. The flow of this water is the flow of wisdom. It's the cycle of life's ceaseless collapse of the known to embody a creativity of extended inspiration and love. Only after surrender of the known can wisdom's passion propel itself forward into time to radiate its presence as physical form. Will I trust this wisdom?"

"You like my painting?" It was Brother Tom. I turned around with a smile, noticing the others still on the other side of the room, absorbed in sharing their observations.

"I do. I learned of these lakes in a mythology class, but now I can feel their energy in your painting. It's odd how Lake Rakshastal feels as pure as its partner lake given that the gods thought of it as the 'Demon Lake'."

"I lived in a monastery by Lake Manasarovar. Every day, we took a bath in its purifying waters. We thought Lake Rakshastal held evil spirits and stayed away. We didn't want its curse. But in my thirties, the winds brought the smell of its saltwater, telling me it had wisdom to share if I visited. I thought it was the whisper of the lake's evil temptress and ignored the message. But its saltwater smell grew ever stronger, even though it was summer, and the mountain winds were still."

"Why not come for one visit and then decide if I am evil?" the soft winds said. "Are you so gullible that you give truth to the opinions of others? They could be wrong."

"I had to admit there was the slightest chance I was misled. So, one day, I went to the lake and told no one where I went. I had been up most of the night doing chores to be free the next day, and I was tired. As I began my trip, gentle winds carried the saltwater smell to me, and I felt less tired. When I got to Lake Rakshastal, its beauty took my breath away. Its tranquil, blue waters met the searing, blue sky. The white stones of its shore looked like fluffy, white clouds that touched the Earth to rest upon its surface. I felt the passionate will of its dark, red island inviting me to share what it had to offer. Free of monks bathing and performing ceremonies around its edges, it was peaceful. I felt no evil, only a sacred silence. I went to this lake every week for a month not saying a word to anyone. But suspicion of my whereabouts grew, and my elder wanted an answer."

"Lake Rakshastal is filled with evil spirits. It will curse you and our monastery. You must stop your trips. I will not allow it," the elder commanded when I told him where I had been.

"Knowing only obedience, I followed his command. But after two weeks, I could no longer ignore the lake's calling. I was even dreaming of it. I told my elder I was being called to the lake, and I must return. If he wanted me to leave the monastery, I would. The elder saw the importance of my need and did not want to step in the way of my spiritual growth. It would bring him very bad karma."

"You may go for now. But if you become ill in body or mind, you will leave here. I do not want others to know where you are. It would create suspicion and arguments. You will give a message to someone who lives a short way from the lake each week to provide an explanation for your absence. Spend no more than two hours at the lake to lessen suspicion."

"I did as he said every week for over two years. My health improved. The elder noted my good health but never said a word. One day as I meditated on the lake's shore, a large, evil-looking, brown face arose from the lake. It was the devil. Its opened mouth proudly revealed its fangs. Its head wore a crown of skeletons that looked like clowns laughing at me."

"Aren't you worn out from your solemn meditations? You put so much effort into hiding your most primitive impulses trying to be the good, holy monk you think yourself to be," the devilish face scoffed at me. "I dare you, brother, to make yourself naked and see what shames you. Run through my water naked, screaming as loud as you can, cursing as the need comes, and cut away your pretense. Recognize your demons, feel your demons, love your demons, and integrate their energy as a part of your Beingness. Allow your soul to transmute their poison into nectar through its love and no longer allow your unresolved impulses to rule you through fear. Imagine yourself free of your fearful demons and be free. You are ready to claim freedom from the shame you have clung to, and suffered from, for so long. Play with me, now!"

"The ugly face dissolved into the lake. I would usually run from such a figure, believing myself belittled and tempted into evil by the devil. But my heart had opened to the lake's spirit, and I felt a truth in the words. I didn't run. I did as the devil asked. I danced naked, emptying rules of correct and incorrect behavior into its deep, blue waters. Every week, I played with the devil as I ran naked through the lake. My awareness was expanding into my most primitive impulses, and I screeched at the top of my lungs to bring them forth to be witnessed. The devil never showed itself again, but I felt its growing joy in the laughter we shared as I ran through its salty waters. When not at the lake, memories causing me shame and guilt came. I recognized and embraced them no matter how unworthy of love I felt.

"Time lost importance, and I lost track of it but was always careful not to miss my day at the lake. One day, I didn't feel like getting naked and running through the water. Instead, I sat by the lake, my lightened heart talking with it. A feeling of deep bliss grew, and the fluffy clouds of its shoreline lifted while carrying me over the lake. Freed of my body, I was my spirit uniting with the lake's spirit. I was in such an exalted state of blissful awareness that I wanted to ascend this Earth and not return into my physical body. But I was asked to remain on this planet to help seed this light into Earth's body if I was willing to do so. After returning to my physical body, the Buddha arose from the lake. Ah, such exquisite beauty! I laid on the sand to breathe Buddha's love inside me. As this deep love expanded, I knew this beauty was not the Buddha's, but my own. My peace was seldom disturbed after that union. When monks spoke of the peace they felt from me, I bowed to them in silence." He became silent.

"Did you tell the elder what you experienced?"

"No, it was too sacred to speak about, and he never inquired about it."

"But wouldn't it help the other monks to know of the lake's sanctity to end their ignorance of its evilness?"

"Good question, but the telling of my story wouldn't end anyone's ignorance. In fact, it would add to it. When I felt my soul's sacredness as a part of me, I knew the lake wasn't the cause of magic. Magic was always inside me. Lake Rakshastal called me because I was ready to know my inner devil. Its spirit took the form of the devil only when I was ready to accept and embrace my darkest demons. It became Buddha only when I was ready to accept the loving wisdom of my own soul and spirit. I had to know a deep love for me, as I was, to accept the love of my sacred Self and integrate it as a facet of my own Beingness. The monks were not ready to acknowledge and embrace their dark demons. If I took them to the lake, they would only distract themselves with rituals and not hear the lake's wisdom. Their demons would remain, and they would find another object to place them upon."

"But the elder knew where you were going. Why didn't he acknowledge the lake's magic?"

"Yes, he did see my deepening peace. But existing within his mind's fears, he was blind to his soul's innocence that could accept the evil lake as the holy magician of love. The elder decided it was my long walks that gave me so much peace, and he walked each day. Jealousy began to stir among the monks. They wanted to deliver the message to know my peace. The elder told me the visits must end, and the next day, I left the monastery. I attempted to live at other monasteries, but I could no longer tolerate their rules. About six months later, as I was heading to a cave in the mountains, I met a monk who had recently inherited this farm from his uncle. I walked with him through the mountains for about a week. As I started to part on my separate way, he asked if I would like to join him in the states. He could use my help. Slowly, other monks found their way here, all with their own stories, but all with the desire to leave the monastery."

When he stopped talking, I pictured this peaceful monk running through the lake naked while screaming curses and started to laugh. He had reclaimed the innocence of his early youth, screeching with its uncontained joy. And it was this loving joy he now radiated that had transformed his demons into love. The others were just catching up to us as I was laughing.

"I shared a tale of a monk I knew when he visited the crescent lake in the painting. It's a private tale between Dakari and me," he said in a quiet, respectful voice.

"This monk is uniquely special. He knows true joy, just as Antonio and Micaela do, but each through their own unique form," I thought to myself. Breathing deeply into this joy, I imagined myself with him often, and I knew it would be.

I bought the small painting of the lakes, and Margaret and Shaun bought the painting I had looked at of this farm in autumn. They loved the fall colors here but couldn't get away from their busy work schedule to visit the northeast during the later fall. They said in their imaginations, the leaf colors were a rainbow in a different form. While he was boxing the gifts, Ethan asked if he would share why he called himself Brother Tom.

"Many people ask about my name. There was a wise, but unknown spirit at a lake that I grew to love. One day, it showed itself in a form and called me 'brother'. I knew that name was used in the states for religious men who had not been ordained. I'm not a religious man, as such, but I am of spirit. When I explored American names, I found Tom meant innocence and simplicity, and both traits felt to describe me."

I chuckled once again as he spoke. "Who would ever guess the spirit's form was the devil, and he took on his dare? Life is an adventure to experience its Mystery! What's next?" I thought with amusement.

We had planned to look at the cashmere products but were hungry and needed downtime after looking at the paintings. We stopped in town to eat and shared how deeply the paintings spoke to us. We never did make it back to the farm that day. The paintings left us with much to absorb for some time.

Two days later, we went to the big city to take in a Broadway show and view the Christmas decorations. I had decided to return to my apartment, rather than the house, at day's end. The space with Antonio's carvings was replacing the garden as my sacred space, and I missed not being in its presence. While I understood that ultimately, sacredness was within, I continued to need the support of the carvings to help center myself in stillness. If I lost myself to drama, I no longer felt my soul's presence. It was not of the world's dense energy and would not engage with it. I had not realized how easily my mind could get enamored by the world's constant drama. My mind was anxious with the changes, and it tried to entice me with distractions. Often, for short periods of time, it worked.

My last semester would start in two weeks, and I wanted to get a couple of applications out to other orchestras should Vermont fall through. I talked to Ethan and Iris once over the past two weeks. I didn't share Brother Tom's story, but I did say that his ability to laugh at himself was a constant reminder about taking my human self too seriously.

Ethan said he's feeling encouraged about changes he wants to make in his music. "When I'm attuned to the vibrations flowing from my violin, the notes seem to direct their own path of becoming. I continue to notice how much force I was asserting to control my endless mind chatter and how that force was diminishing my music's depth. The more I breathe compassion through me, the more I hear the subtle resonance the notes want to sing," he said in a voice that continued to soften. "I stopped writing notes for now because I noticed when I did, my mind tended to interfere. I never thought I'd appreciate free time as I now do. It's freeing me of my need to always accomplish something. I had sought a carrot's bait that teased me with its promise of harmony ahead, but it was one of my many trappings into the misery of false hope."

Iris said the shawl was keeping her so warm, she's spending more time in the garden this winter than she ever had. "The angel appreciates having her feet washed in warm, herbal waters every day. I feel its profound, sacred love. It's not so easy to stay in that love once I leave the angel's presence, but each day gets a little easier. It feels odd to accept that I'm more than my human self. It's going to take some time."

I laughed, agreeing that nothing about this work is easy, but also recognizing the beauty I felt when I did allow my soul's presence. I said the angel is meant to serve her now.

"The angel has always served me but in a different way. It helped to give me strength to raise you while keeping me from falling into despair at times. But I agree it can serve me more intimately now only because I'm ready for it to do so. Its support will be especially helpful because Antonio sent a note to tell us he'll be leaving in three months. He wants time to travel but also believes his assistance would only get in the way now. He said Micaela was available for support, and he needed to move on."

I said I had a feeling he would be leaving soon and agreed his absence would be an adjustment. I would also miss him.

FIFTEEN

I received an invitation for an audition with the Vermont Symphony Orchestra a couple of days after the semester began. It was scheduled for mid-February. I was provided with two musical scores I had never played. I did not use my new instruments at college, as I did not want the attention they would call. But I savored practicing with them at my place. While I looked forward to sharing their unique sound at my audition, I knew what was most important was the space my breath originated from. "Breathe from the stillness of my center," I kept reminding myself while practicing. "Do not allow outside energies to taint the sound."

When I called Ethan and Iris to tell them about the interview, they asked for Micaela's email after congratulating me. They needed support with the changes taking place in themselves and in their relationship. I did not feel the need to contact Micaela.

"Perhaps Micaela was merely a bridge, a crossover from my former life into my new life," I thought. Recalling the connection Iris and Ethan felt to her ballad, even before meeting Micaela, I knew I was also a bridge that brought her to them.

Brother Tom's painting was magically blending with the energy of Antonio's carvings, and both called my attention to them often. I was feeling the pulsing flow of Lake Rakshastal move through the serpents' bodies with increasing intensity. Daily, I asked the lake and the serpents to tell me of the Mystery they held. One evening while falling into sleep, the whispering winds that stroked the lake's surface spoke, "Feel my love, breathe my love, be my love." Losing myself to the dreamworld as I allowed the lake's breath of love to meld with my breath, Lake Rakshastal appeared, a mist rising from its surface. I felt to exist as the cumulus cloud that perched over my body resting on its shore. A dark, heavy, threatening cloud hovered nearby as if awaiting its moment to strike me down into density with its fearful, abrasive presence.

The serpents of the angel's pedestal emerged from within the lake's mist, their forms barely distinguishable from the Light Aura they emitted. Misty droplets, reflecting this light, shimmered as crystals. "Dakari, do you still not know who You are? Do you not yet realize You are the Pure Consciousness that assumes any form it wishes to assume?" their searing, black eyes asked gravely through their telepathic vibrations. "The outer skin of our physical form continually sheds its decayed life to be renewed in new life. Yet, we know no fear, as we embody the life power of our eternal spirit within our bottomless, sacred center. Our raw, eternal passion is terrifying only if you resist the death of who you have known yourself to be. The dark cloud hovering about is the darkness of your mind's fear to surrender its controlling life force. Only your soul's love can dissipate its foreboding energy. When will you choose to embrace fear as the harmless beast of your mind's duality and its judgment? When will you just be done with empowering its ruffle of illusion?"

As the serpents dissolved into the mist, my cloud form inhaled the exquisite love of the remaining shimmering crystals. Exhaling my gentle wind, my fluffy mass of water droplets was lifted even higher. The dark cloud blew its breath of fury as it moved closer. I felt the raw power of its lightning bolts preparing to strike me down while emptying its heavy waters into my rising cloud. I stilled all movement, losing my presence to the passionate love illuminating my hollow, feathery form. I inhaled my breath full in love, then exhaled a compassionate breeze in the direction of the cloud. "Rain on me as you wish, my misguided partner," I whispered through my light wind. "I know your droplets to be of love. Your darkest depths are the radiant sacredness of life's dark Mystery, and I claim the life force of my sacred Self hidden within your dark depths. I will no longer relate to your darkness through fear."

I awoke to a gentle breeze caressing my face. Slowly becoming aware of my body and seeing the room's window closed to keep out the mid-winter chill, my dream returned. Realizing this breeze to be the touch of my soul, I opened every fiber of my being to absorb its presence within me. Passionate love exploded through my cells as it lifted my awareness into a state of bliss-filled love. There was no need to leave my body; my soul was integrating its sacredness within the fibers of my Beingness. "The full integration of my crystalline energy will take time," I sensed my soul's light say to my body. "I don't want to burn your biological body into ashes by asking it to integrate the totality of my love before it is prepared to do so. Just keep breathing increasing depths of my awareness through your beingness each day. I'll do the work of transmuting your biology."

I practiced for the audition as often as I could. Moving ever deeper into a trusting surrender of my sacred presence, my notes soared on golden wings, then dispersed their light into the space of their origin. A balance between my mind's presence as the master of technique, and my soul's presence as the master of passionate creativity, was evolving. I was ready for the audition when the time arrived. I stayed in Westchester the night before. Only Antonio was home when I arrived. Ethan and Iris were at a theater event.

"Dakari, wonderful to see you, especially the You that's glowing in light. Beautiful."

I smiled as my heart silently shared its love, and Antonio's dark eyes gleamed with joy. I became the magical presence of my childhood self, appreciating the enchanting glow beaming through every fiber of Antonio's Beingness. In the pure beauty shared, I almost lost my footing from the dizziness that came over me.

"Why don't you put your things in your room while I make your cappuccino?" he offered. "I'd love to spend time with you."

After putting my things in my room, I splashed water on my face. I needed the grounding cold water provided. When I returned to the kitchen, Antonio had made lunch for both of us.

"I'm ahead of myself getting things ready for dinner. How about we take lunch into the sunroom and relax?"

It was a sunny day. Brother Tom's painting hung on the wall opposite Antonio's carvings, alive with the sun's joy. It was the first time I saw the painting since Christmas, and the energy it radiated deeply moved me. Remembering Brother Tom's story, I started to chuckle.

"I'm recalling a private story Brother Tom, the painting's artist, told me about a painting of his I bought for my place. I haven't shared it with anyone, but I don't feel I'm violating his confidence to share it with you."

"I know Brother Tom well," Antonio said through his chuckles when I finished. "He has a couple of my carvings, and I have a couple of his paintings. We've enjoyed exchanging crafts our souls express their passion through. I've never seen your painting, but he did share the story long ago, and I enjoyed listening to it again. We've shared many stories of our inner journeys, and our laughter at what we once took so seriously. Meeting and befriending our inner devil helped us to leave fear to experience a playful joy that had been absent."

I described the painting I had bought, and my dream with the dark cloud.

"I didn't know the specifics, but the glow you now radiate told me you had embraced a darkness that was holding you back. You're well on your way to embodying your soul. It does take time to integrate its crystalline energy due to changes in your biology that are necessary to accommodate its intense light. The light infused into your awareness at your birth is greatly assisting and accelerating this transformation. However, necessary changes in your biology remain."

"I've been told my memories won't be lost, but I'm unsure what will happen to my mind's life force."

"Your mind is a necessary aspect to being human. But the more your mind yields to the beauty it feels radiating from your soul, the more it can adapt to its new role as a partner to it. Continue to accept your mind through your soul's love as you're already doing. Your mind's thoughts are already growing quiet as they lose their charge."

"I enjoyed Brother Tom and want to visit him sometime soon."

"Listen to your intuition and trust it. It's the voice of your soul. Brother Tom won't tell you what to think or do, but he openly shares his wisdom and love with those able to be touched by it. He shared his story only because he recognized your readiness to receive the sacred essence it holds. Already you've benefited from it."

I was tired when I finished eating and told Antonio I needed to rest before dinner. My room, my sanctuary I had known for so long, felt oddly foreign. My inner changes were changing my outer world. My mind, the foundation that once supported my existence, *was* yielding to the support my soul offered. Putting my head on the pillow, I recalled the challenge of Lake Rakshastal's spirit to Brother Tom to rid himself of his pretensions. My mind had its own pretense that only it knew what was best. It feared losing relevance if the wisdom of my soul and spirit was integrated. But I knew with certainty that in time, my mind would no longer doubt its importance as a partner to my sacred Self.

I had fallen into a deep sleep and was awakened by Ethan's voice telling me dinner was ready. Antonio had left a couple of hours before and left dinner warming. When Ethan called, his voice was free of the demand I often sensed to stop what I'm doing, now, and come to dinner. His presence was continuing to soften, and every fiber of his being was responding to this softening. Dinner was buffet style, and they had just started eating. Iris got up to give her usual warm hug, again congratulating me on the audition with Ethan echoing her excitement.

"I took the car for a checkup to be sure it's ready for the trip," Ethan said. "Some maintenance work was done, and it's all set for you."

I nodded my appreciation for his gesture of support, then talked about the musical scores I would play. "I've practiced grounding my breath into my center where my nerves can't touch the sacred sound that I want to share. I sense my new instruments embracing my breath as their notes soar through the air when released from them. I'm looking forward to sharing our blended sound at my audition."

Ethan talked about how he continued to benefit from Micaela's music as he expanded ever deeper into the still space that she created from. The passion he had known at my birth was slowly becoming present to him once again. But this time, he could relate to the energy with increasing ease and comfort. It was feeling far less foreign.

"Are you still creating music with your computer?"

"I am. I'm not yet ready to leave it completely behind. Perhaps it will always remain to some degree, but in a different form. As I play my violin, new musical patterns are emerging. In the future, I'll most likely feed them into my computer to share them. But I will not use my computer to generate new music from the patterns I feed it. It would taint the music's initial purity. I'm sensing a growing attunement to the creative depths of musicians and what motivates their sound. If their motivations are of fame and money, I'm letting them go. Perhaps artists of greater depth will be attracted to me. You're not in college anymore and there's plenty to hold us over for quite some time as I move through these changes. I won't rush what can't be rushed."

"But isn't it possible that other artists will take your patterns and use their computers to replicate them? It's getting easier to do that with advancements in digital technology. I'm a little concerned about others replicating my music through software programs in the future."

"It is possible musical engineers will record my original patterns and create from them. Their actions can't be controlled, but their work will lack the inspiration of true creativity. Their music may inspire the whims of minds, but it cannot touch the space of spirit's inspiration. It's a trivial sound I'll no longer help to create and support."

I heard Ethan's trust in his decisions and understood his choices. I assured them there's no need for their financial help. I wanted to be on my own after college, and I would have no difficulty getting paid work for various musical engagements until full-time work came.

"We see that strength in you, and we're grateful because your independence does offer us freedom," Iris said through a voice growing in strength and confidence. "We were busy at the theater all afternoon. Ethan offered his violin talents for our current production. Last year, we started writing a play about gods and goddesses with androgenous natures. With all the changes in our culture, and people's lack of comfort with many of them, we wanted to make others aware that even some deities were bisexual. We may lose a few of our regulars, but the great majority wanted to go ahead with the play. We've developed the reputation of raising controversial issues, so we doubt few will leave. And if they do, others will come to fill their space.

"I'm excited about this play because I'm better sensing the sacred Male energies I embody. I was blind to the protection I sought from Ethan and the sacred passion I was suffocating that would initiate deep transformation. As I increasingly feel my soul's presence, I sense its wisdom reminding me that no one outside of my sacred Self is needed for protection or inner transformation. I want to act through its expression, not my mind's outworn emotions that I've habitually expressed as representing me and my characters. I could never go back to those days."

"Was there any particular character you wanted to act?" I asked out of curiosity.

"We decided to bring 10 deities to life, each of a different mythological tradition. I'm playing Venus Barbata, a deity the ancient Romans worshipped as an epithet of the goddess Venus. It's the goddess Venus with a beard and body of a male, but with female robing. It was thought that sometimes the goddess became a god, and at other times, the god became a goddess. While I must remain true to the mythology of that time, I know that beyond the form of male or female attire and body is the core of Venus Barbata that sees through the illusion of positive or negative charges being dominant at any one point in time. I sometimes wear the beard at home, imagining my own truth that doesn't engage in oppositional forces and their tensions. The beard is helping to free myself from an identity that had become suffocating."

Iris left the table and returned, fully bearded. I laughed but became silent when she began to speak through a deeply passionate voice, full of strength. "I am Venus Barbata." Hands holding her long, loose top out slightly, she continued, "I am the goddess of beauty, understanding, and love." Moving her hands over her beard she stated, "I am the god of protection and action." Bringing her right hand to her heart, and her left hand to her navel area she said, "But my truth is the Pure Consciousness that birthed both. I am with form, and formless, at the same time. I am my eternal Self as spirit, my intuitive Self as soul, and my human self as mind and body. I am shedding my heavily burdened and decayed layer of skin to realize immortality while still in human form."

Ethan and I clapped. "Wow, the Iris and Ethan I once knew are but shadow figures now," I thought. I spontaneously found myself saying, "I understand the need to act your characters that's true to their mythology, but perhaps in the future, your group could write a play that extends the understanding of gods and goddesses. What you just acted does answer some questions basic to mythology: Who am I? Where did I come from? Why am I here? What is existence? Perhaps you will seed new ideas and questions in the audience if others agree to this."

Iris was nodding in agreement. "Not such a bad idea. I'll see if others are interested."

"I agree," Ethan said. "You've made me aware I had accepted what I was taught as the only truth about the gods and goddesses, closing my imagination to new ideas. Maybe you could do the same for others. I'm starting to think that most of what I've believed to be true is quite limited and misguided. I suppose I had to be willing to open my eyes to allow the flaws of my beliefs to be seen."

SIXTEEN

I was up long before daylight the next morning, the house still. My footsteps, breaking through the icy, crusted snow beneath a blanket of clouds hiding the moon's glow, announced my presence to the predawn darkness. I had befriended what I once scorned, now knowing that beneath the drapery of winter's bitter, dark nights and days, the seeds of renewed life germinated. I was ready to embrace the adventures ahead that my spirit's passion summoned from within my soul's dark womb. My audition would be at a concert hall in a small city in the northeast corner of Vermont. I had listened to concerts at this historical center many times before. Loving care and attention had been given to the preservation of the building's artistry, and the best acoustics available occupied its chambers. The opportunity to play my new instruments there excited me. I had prepared well, imagining my sound soaring through its majestic hall. "I've already created what I'll share," I reassured myself.

I drove the backroads through small, quaint towns. Halfway to my destination, I entered Vermont where a small café caught my attention. Just opening its doors, it was yet to experience the lively chatter of local customers. The unrushed, friendly pace made my drive even more relaxing. I arrived a couple of hours early. I needed time for the warmup, but I had over an hour free prior to entering the building. There was a museum nearby that displayed exhibitions of local artists. The crafts echoed the artists' deep connection to nature's soul, and they would help relax any anxieties that fear attempted to tease in me.

A quilt exhibit was on display this time. Each quilt was an abstract color scheme of an element in nature, and the viewer was challenged to identify its element. This task was more difficult than it would seem, as every element changed color during Vermont's seasonal changes, and most of nature's elements shared similar colors. The more I tuned into the color vibrations each quilt emitted, the more accurate I became. Did the vibrations carry the flow of a river, the whisper of the wind, the brittleness of ice? It was an unexpected warmup that helped me center within a space that knew no distractions. I took one more deep breath before leaving, opening to the collective symphony the quilts sang while imbibing nature's passion to share its majesty through my music. I was relaxed, and I was ready.

After introducing myself at the front desk, I was led to a room to prepare. Even the practice room of this preserved building announced its grandeur: its high ceiling in expectation of the sound it would embrace as I played. My music would live on within the building, blending with the endless sounds its fibers had absorbed over the years. Breathing the room's energy into my being, I invited its splendor to blend with my sound in whatever way it chose. As I played, my breath surrendered ever more deeply into the room's enchanting spell. My fingers danced upon my flute and piccolo as gold and silver rays of light spiraled out of their hollow centers into the ceiling's heights, then returned to their source to create a new dance. I heard a knock and was told five minutes remained prior to being taken to the audition. Light encased me in its protective shell as I stood. "Hold what you now embody. Do not allow distraction to taint the sound's purity," the room's magic spoke as its light accompanied me to the space of my audition.

I have only vague memories of my audition. After taking my place on stage, a handful of seated adults introduced themselves. They said my audition would be recorded, and I would be sent a digital copy. I placed my music on the stand, breathed my spirit's passion into my center, and brought my flute to my mouth. I felt bliss, breathed bliss, and surrendered into bliss. As I played, the protective shell of light about me expanded, carrying my breath deep into the hollow chambers of my body. Transmuting my breath into sound, my instruments filled the room's chambers with their vibrations. I was a cumulus cloud, lifting and expanding into the spaciousness of the high ceilings. At the same time, I was my body, holding my instrument to my mouth as my fingers flowed over its keyholes. There was no need to think about how to play the notes or what notes to play. I had practiced so much that my mind and fingers knew what to do. I merely had to trust my human self as it directed the mechanics of the notes, and my soul Self as it directed the resonance of the notes, and I trusted both. My spirit, soul, and human mind, completely in sync, played the musical score before me. Even the transitions between my flute and piccolo, and the two musical scores, were seamless.

Becoming aware the second score would soon end, I slowly brought my full awareness into my body. When the sound ended, the people in the room stood to applaud. "Bravo, bravo!" they voiced with great excitement. "That was superb! I believe you'll be hearing good news from us shortly. We have a handful of auditions left, and you will receive our decision by the middle of next week." After a slight bow, I left the stage.

I was grateful I had put boots in my car. I needed the cold, crisp air that a walk in Vermont's bitter cold would provide. While there was always a part of me wanting to question the magic that was increasingly showing itself, my mind had to acknowledge the vibrant aliveness this magic engendered. Its deep, sensuous passion, and the world it was creating, was beginning to feel more real than the world my mind knew when it refused to allow this creative passion. I could no longer live in a world devoid of the love that magic lived within. The laws of the mind, that deadened magic, were beginning to feel alien.

I stopped for lunch at a café I had enjoyed on previous visits. The weather remained cooperative, so I decided to take the backroads again. Driving through an area not far from where Brother Tom lived, I knew I would soon visit him. Perhaps he would enjoy listening to my audition. I had not yet checked if it was sent. Ethan had the best sound equipment money could buy, and I did not want to tempt myself with listening to it until I could use his equipment.

There was a note saying they were doing errands when I got to Westchester and would buy dinner on their way home. Finding the recording sent, I went to Ethan's studio to listen. I attempted to relax my nerves as I sunk into the chair's soft cushion. "Wow, I'm really nervous. I suppose the truth to my music's sound is about to make itself known."

The tape began with the introduction of the judges. I differentiated three females and two males from their names and voices, details that had escaped me before. They were all business in their introductions: respectful, but aloof at the same time. "Completely objective to what they were about to hear," I thought. In the still silence that followed, I heard my deep breaths, and I was taking those same deep breaths now. My flute broke through the air's anticipation, singing a pure, pristine sound, and I attuned to the song of my spirit's passion and my soul's love. Within the space of my closed eyes, I saw my body on stage playing my flute. The gold and silver spirals of light reappeared, and the silhouettes of the serpents' bodies were faintly visible within them. Ascending into the ceilings, the spirals expanded and merged, then contracted and separated as they descended into my flute, seeming to have become the other. Their joyful dance felt explosive with the desire to create music.

My breath deepened into this passion, and the high ceilings opened as if to allow the light to soar beyond its structure. My breath was one with my spirit's breath of light as it expanded and contracted effortlessly within the multidimensions of the universe. I was of the physical dimension of time and space while also of the subtle dimensions unconstrained by linear time and space. I was light, breathing light. My physical body holding my instrument was a mere shadow. Toward the end of the second score, as I was bringing my awareness back into my body, the building's soul spoke, "We have great times ahead. Your audition is only the beginning of our new venture." I knew I had the job. It was just a matter of my acceptance letter manifesting in this physical reality. I made a handful of copies and was just finishing when Ethan came into the studio.

"Hi. I was just finishing making some copies of my audition for you and a few others. I'm really exhausted and hungry now, so do you mind waiting to hear it?"

"Sounds good. We're also tired and hungry. It's better to listen tomorrow when we're rested. How'd the audition go?"

"You'll see for yourself tomorrow, but I'm quite sure I'll be offered the job. I feel good about how everything went."

Ethan congratulated me as we headed to the house, and Iris did the same when I shared my news. As we ate, I offered little about my audition except that I was very centered and not affected by my nerves. I did describe the museum exhibit and suggested a visit when they had time. Iris said the "right" moment to talk about my suggestion for the new play hadn't come up. Most likely, she'd wait until after the current production when new ideas could be better listened to and considered.

I headed to bed after dinner and woke up early the next day. Antonio wasn't here, as a blizzard was due to arrive in the early afternoon. After a quick breakfast, I got my things together to return to the city. Ethan was up by then and gave me a lift to the train station. I was looking forward to getting home to its welcoming energy. I realized I would miss my apartment when I moved to Vermont. "Everything is so vibrant with life," I thought. "Buildings do vibrate with the energies of those who have shared its space. I'm going to fill my new home with energies of great peace."

My acceptance letter arrived the week after my audition. I shared the letter and a digital copy of my audition with my orchestra teacher. He called me to him when I entered class the following day. "Dakari, I've never heard such pure sound from a student. I seldom hear this quality of sound even from the best professionals. There are some minor issues needing attention, but with experience and maturity, they'll be resolved. I'd like you to play a solo for the spring concert if you're willing. The orchestra will accompany you. I'd be honored as the conductor. It's up to you, no pressure."

I did not hesitate to respond, "It's an opportunity to express my gratitude for all you've shared these past four years. I'd be honored."

The next time the orchestra met, the conductor told them of his plans for the spring concert, and they welcomed his announcement. None had forgotten that magical moment we shared shortly before last semester's end. Some had come to me in the days that followed, thanking me for creating a musical moment that had remained with them. Many later encouraged me to lead them into that moment of magic again as I played my solo at the spring concert.

"Wouldn't it be great if we shared that magical moment with the audience?" the three other flutists said a week later as we were warming up our instruments. "Anything we can do to help ourselves, and you, please let us know."

"All I can offer is that the more deeply you feel the passion the music wishes to express, the more magic it can sing. Expand your breath inward through love, leaving distracting thoughts and emotions behind. When you find that center of complete stillness, breathe this loving passion into your flute. The sorcerer of truly great music is the inspiration found deep within the sacred chambers of your heart. If your mind leads the music, the magic is lost."

What I offered was somewhat similar to what the conductor often told us, so they confidently shook their heads in acknowledgment. "Hmmm," one girl said. "Creating through the heart's passion, free of distraction. I'm with you on that suggestion."

The last semester was proving to be very busy, and four weeks had passed without a visit to Westchester. I spoke to Iris and Ethan twice. They had called the day after I left to share how much they enjoyed my audition. "Now I'll listen to Micaela's ballad, and your audition, every day. Both inspire me to create a sound so pure, so flowing in grace, it can't be imitated. We're so proud of you and honored to have shared the time we have with you," Ethan had said.

"And I'll listen over and over to both as well, absorbing the inspiration that sings through them. You belong to your soul and spirit, Dakari, and you are completely free to do as your sacred Self guides you. Neither of us would ever want to interfere with destiny."

I called a couple of weeks later. They already had a meeting with Micaela and planned to meet every six weeks or so for the next few months. They said Micaela was helping them move through changes in how they understood their own human and spiritual natures. Her compassion enabled candor with the fallacies they unconsciously held on to without offending them. They were better able to embrace their faults as they arose without judgment.

"Antonio's presence is inspiring me not to get discouraged with what can sometimes feel like two steps backward after a step forward," Ethan said. "I'm helping in the kitchen much more than before. Having more time as I let clients go plays into that, but Antonio and I both know my main motivation is to hear his wisdom. I've finally learned that while he'll share his stories, he doesn't want to assume the role of Micaela. He had served a different purpose, preparing us for what we're now entering. So, I'm learning to just relax into the joy of Antonio's presence. Every time I do, I hear a purity sing in my music that I hadn't heard before. I'll miss him, but he's doing exactly what needs to be done for all of us."

I heard Iris sigh deeply before she spoke. "I can't think

about him leaving, but I agree it's best for all. Antonio asked that I wash the angel when he's not around. He wants to phase out my dependency on him. He said the angel wants to be filled with my soul, not his. Each time gets a little easier. I can't be the Venus Barbata I've come to appreciate if I don't fully embrace my inner strength."

I heard another sigh of resignation. Change had been activated and resistance would only cause suffering. I shared my experience with the soul of the concert hall, reminding them that Antonio's presence was weaved within the soul of their home and garden. "I'm finding that when I allow my soul's presence to be me, I can relate to Antonio anywhere. His soul, like all souls, transcends time and space. I don't need to be in his physical presence to feel his support."

"Antonio's spirit was always lifting my awareness to feel his joy. An immeasurable gift," Iris said through yet another sigh. "Have you felt the need to talk to Micaela as we have?"

"No, but I'd like to see Brother Tom this coming weekend. I'll be home early Friday evening, and on my way early Saturday morning with my trusted car. When I called, he said business remains slow after Christmas, and he'd enjoy my visit. I think I was meant to bring Micaela to you and Ethan, more than to myself."

"We're nodding our agreement on our end," Ethan said. "She's the right person for both of us now. We have a commitment Friday night and won't be home until late. Let us know if you'll be home for dinner Saturday as your day progresses."

"Will do. See you sometime Saturday."

$\smile\!\!\!\infty$

SEVENTEEN

It was early evening when I got to Westchester, and the house was quiet. I went right to bed, setting the alarm for 5:00 a.m. before falling off to sleep. I didn't want to oversleep and miss time with Brother Tom. He had said early mornings were best, as customers tended to wait until the later hours of the morning to come. It was mid-March, and the bitter winds of the northeast winter were yielding to the warming winds of the lengthening daylight sun. Icy roads and dangerous snow squalls were highly unlikely, and the drive would be easy. So, I decided to take the backroads.

I stopped at a café halfway there, already busy with what appeared to be regular customers welcomed with their names. Its atmosphere was an extreme contrast to the city. I realized how urban my life had become over the past four years and that living in a much smaller city could be a difficult adjustment. I had grown to appreciate the anonymity a large city offered but also needed the country. Without the house in Westchester to escape to, I wouldn't have been able to cope with the constant noise and activity. "It'll work out," I assured myself. "I found a balance before, and I'll find it again. It's just a matter of time and acclimation."

I arrived at the farm before business hours, but there was no problem driving into the visitor's parking lot. "They attract only what needs to be here," I thought. "Drama doesn't enter a place where it can't find energy to feed on." The goats were out for an early morning walk, most likely soaking up any warmth the air was now befriending. I knocked, then entered the waiting room. Brother Tom appeared at his open studio door and invited me in. There was a small, wooden table and two chairs near the space of the large window. A thermos and two ceramic cups, each with a closed lotus painted on the side, as well as honey and milk, rested on the table.

"Would you like a cup of hot, black tea?" he asked through a gentle smile in his eyes and around his mouth.

"I'd love some."

Once we sat, his full attention was given to the task of pouring tea. Gently taking the thermos into his hand, he barely touched its lid to unscrew it as if the lid responded to his intention. Released from his hand a couple of inches from the tabletop, the lid defied gravity, gliding to the table's surface and softly resting upon it. Flowing toward my cup, the tea's dark liquid transformed into droplets of crystalline light. My cup's lotus vibrated with life, opening to receive the falling crystal droplets. He handed me my cup as if what I had just witnessed was perfectly normal. Although I typically added honey and milk, I didn't want to disturb its crystalline light. Yet, the tea tasted as if I had added both. Even the nectar of my fine birthday wine waned to what I now experienced.

Without adding anything to his cup, Brother Tom silently sipped his tea while looking out the window. I did the same. Initially, I felt uneasy in the silence, but the aroma of the tea enticed my entire mind and body to relax. Through slow, deep breaths I filled my cells with the tea's relaxing aroma. Sipping more of its sweet nectar, the entire room became vividly alive. The vibrations of various colored paints called my attention, first singing their unique song, followed by their unified symphony. "The pure vibrations of the rainbow, the cosmic mind, are sharing their pure delight," I thought while welcoming every nuance of their individual and unified songs.

I dreamily discerned Brother Tom's voice through the silence. I thought I had fallen into a light sleep, but my cup was empty. I was wide awake, but I was awake to an entirely different reality that defied laws perceived by the human mind such as gravity. As in my audition, I was acting through my body, but at the same time, immersed in the sensuousness of the experience through the space of my divine imagination. And within that space of awareness, physical form readily transformed itself through the energy that created and supported its existence. Brother Tom's eyes were open as he began to speak, but he was not inviting eye contact.

"We have three cars that 13 monks share, so it's not often I can visit places alone. But when I do, I enjoy going to a town where I'm unknown. I visit craft stores and eat at local cafés that are usually filled. I sense immense distraction and worry that keeps the pain in human hearts hidden. Their unspoken pain feels louder than their spoken chatter. I became a monk because I needed the quiet to hear my soul speak. But even life on this farm has its daily challenges that can upset quiet. If my mind is heavy with thoughts, the quiet here is hidden, just as it is hidden from most who visit. It's not easy to meet and accept our inner devil, especially when you know that if it gets placed onto another there will be more suffering. Each time I accept a dark shadow within, the magic of sacred love expands in everything I do."

"I'm just now becoming aware of the chatter I entered with. Your tea ritual distracted me from my distractions. I'm glad I released my worries to witness your subtle magic. I'm most attentive to distracting thoughts and emotions when I create music because I'm aware of how they taint the purity of the sound I want to inspire others with. I auditioned with the Vermont Symphony

Orchestra about a month ago. It was a magical moment when I felt completely centered in my soul and spirit, and I was offered the job. I have the disc with me if you'd like to listen."

His appreciative eyes accepted my disc, and he put it in a small recorder. Returning to his seat he closed his eyes, and I did the same. Shortly after the music started, his painting of Lake Manasarovar, with its vortex, appeared. The white flame of my previous visions, its gray luster at its center, hovered over the vortex. The flame's form transmuted into a white stallion ablaze in the wildness of its untamed spirit, and its gray eyes emanated wisdom's brilliance. Its majestic presence stirred the waters of the vortex beneath it. I felt the stirring of my own dark depths as they expanded to receive the stallion's passion. Taking a deep, slow breath, Lake Rakshastal appeared as I exhaled.

"Dakari, you have done well," its winds whispered. "Your heart now knows the blissful union of sacred Masculine and Feminine energies that do not engage in the charged tension of your mind's inner battles. Be aware through this loving passion as often as you can. Your mind is accepting your soul's presence more than it ever had before."

The form of Lake Rakshastal gave way to a translucent rainbow shortly before the music of my audition ended. Some time passed before Brother Tom turned the recorder off. I slowly opened my eyes. He poured the remains of the tea into my cup. The flow of the tea was the flow of a rainbow.

"Magnificent music. Your spirit was soaring. This copy is for me?"

I nodded a yes.

"Thank you. I will listen to your music often as I paint. It will inspire me. Enjoy your tea. I have things to do in another building. Let yourself out when done. You took in much light, and your mind and body aren't as quick to react. I suggest you take a long walk on the grounds before driving. The monks know you're here and will give you the space and time you need. Visit as you like, just let me know of your plans first."

I nodded, and he left. Savoring every drop of my tea, I keenly listened to each nuance it sang while absorbing its textured layers into my being. When I went into the outside air, it was still. It did not yet hold the noisy, busy activity of visitors. The trees creaked, stretching their limbs to create space for sap to flow through them. The ground slurped, absorbing the waters of its melting winter blanket. The returning birds sang their unique tunes while also blending to sing a unified concerto of new life. But as people came, nature's voice was masked. It was time to leave. I stopped for lunch in town and texted Ethan that I'd be home for dinner. Tired, I took the highway back while looking forward to not keeping my mind alert to the road.

Ethan was in the kitchen making dinner when I got home, and Iris was out working with the theater group. He poured himself some wine and offered me the same. I gladly accepted it.

"I've spent almost the entire day in this kitchen, relaxing my mind to capture the fullness of Antonio's joy. I usually use measurement tools, but as the afternoon progressed, I increasingly trusted my intuitive sense to guide me. We'll see how dinner tastes, but even if the taste isn't the best, the combined love of Antonio and me is infused into the food. And we all know love is the main ingredient," Ethan lightheartedly added.

I indulged his optimism. "I'm willing to wager it's your best meal ever."

I shared a bit about Brother Tom's magical tea ritual, and the sweetness of the tea despite not putting any sweetener into it. "His magic was so subtle that I would've missed it if my mind was distracted."

Ethan nodded his understanding. "When I bring my awareness back in time to being a kid, freeing myself of my analytical mind, I feel some of the magic I knew. I wasn't even aware of the pain and suffering around me."

Hearing Iris open the garage door, Ethan poured wine for her. It was a label I had not seen before, and I looked more closely at the bottle.

"It's the same wine used for your birthday, but a different brand. It caught my attention at the store, and I bought it. I wanted to make a special dinner to celebrate your new beginning, and the wine seemed to want to join the celebration."

I complimented his choice as Iris walked in. While she spoke words that echoed her usual greeting, the essence those words carried was noticeably different. Her joy was beginning to ground itself in the strength she was claiming, and her voice echoed a deeper trust in herself. Its gentle, but resolute hue warned others she would not allow herself to be mistreated. "She really is embracing a deep appreciation for all parts of herself," I thought.

Dinner really did taste good. "The cooking measurements will have a lot less work to do. I suppose the same holds true for my mind. Challenges abound, but inspiration is also abundant. Why don't you share Brother Tom's tea ritual with Iris?"

As I described his ritual, Ethan listened with even greater attention. I added how even the paints in his studio sang with the vibrations of his magic.

"I've spent much time in the sunroom this winter with his painting. Increasingly, I felt the stallion's passionate strength calling the darkness to it. The love within my own dark, inner chambers responded as I felt its compassion helping me to avoid getting entangled with emotions of past drama. I sense its love dissolving the energies I once gave so much power to while teasing me with the fullness of its love that awaits my embrace. When I soaked my iris seeds recently, I recalled the magic of the angel's scepter that can thaw my hardened wall of resistance. Freeing my mind of its harsh judgment isn't easy, but love's abundance is expanding to do so."

I nodded slightly. "Has Micaela been here to visit again?"

"No, when we decided to work regularly with her, we agreed to keep our relationship formal and have been meeting online. Micaela said she knew she wouldn't be working with you long-term in the same manner that she'd be working with Ethan and myself. Our needs are different from your needs."

"Brother Tom invited me whenever I wanted to visit, and I know I'll be returning often. I'm just now realizing how he works in much the same way Antonio had worked with me all these years. He talks little but emits profound love that touches my inner depths. That touch of love inspires and challenges me to exist within my soul's love without his support."

Iris said Micaela's energy and her verbal guidance were necessary for them, as they would lose their way without both. The beliefs and conditioning of their upbringing continued to need attention. "Our gratitude for Antonio's loving guidance all these years is immense," Iris said. "His presence kept your childhood heart pure. Even during your adolescent years, his joy protected you from the world's harshness. Recently, we shared our depth of gratitude to him, and he responded by sharing his gratitude for the many things he's enjoyed here. 'It was meant to be exactly as it was,' he responded, and we knew he was right."

After dinner, we walked into the garden to look at its early spring life. The angel emitted a strength I was increasingly observing in Iris. I knew its presence was helping Iris to feel her inner strength as it dissolved energies that fed her shame and guilt.

"The angel's energy feels very different. It *is* here to assist you," I said to Iris.

"I know. Even in my dreams, I engage with the angel differently. When its serpents' dark eyes show themselves, I can stop myself from cringing and closing off to what they have to offer. I'm far from ready to embrace their depths, but I can peer into my fears their compassion is bringing to the surface. As I release support from the outer God I once sought, I'm finding faith to allow my inner, sacred Self to cleanse what remains to be cleansed. Such huge changes in all I've known life and myself to be."

"I'm spending much more time in the garden as I get acquainted with its different energy," Ethan said when Iris became silent. "I had memorized the words of your soul, but I recently put them on paper. It was a formal declaration to my mind that it's relieved of its duty to make sense of them, and the garden helps relax my mind's analytical habits. Simple things, like feeling the breeze across my face, watching the melting snow transform its solid form into small streams, and appreciating the sun's warmth after the bitter winter, help to bring a purer presence alive to feel what your soul's words want to share. I also listen to Micaela's ballad here, and your audition as well. A subtle kindling of my own spirit's inspiration burns, full of hope that it will find its way into this world. And I'm committed to do just that. No amount of money or fame could tease a return to my old ways. I'm fully aware of their trappings, and I will not be distracted by them."

The wind was picking up as the sun set, and we headed inside. I hadn't planned to return to my apartment that night, but on a whim, I asked Ethan if he could give me a lift to the train station. Neither asked any questions. I recognized that while we shared the past twenty-one years together, most energies of our biological bonding had dissolved as my bonding with the love of my soul, and the light of my spirit, strengthened. There was more for Ethan and Iris to work through, but that was their work, not mine. They were not yet ready to claim complete sovereignty with their soul and spirit that I was already beginning to embrace. However, the foundation of passionate love to embrace that sovereignty had been

built to varying degrees in them, and regardless of any
challenges ahead, it would not crumble.

EPILOGUE

I'm walking through my garden in Vermont as the last remaining leaves of fall blanket the few remaining flowers that refuse to yield to the teasing touches of frost. It was mid-October, and the howling winds of winter were beginning to stir the air with warnings of their upcoming arrival. Each year over the past four years, my garden had grown in its number of plants, and its depths of peace. Today, Antonio's presence would be planted into its soil. He had been in Florence, Italy, for over three years laying the groundwork for his new café. Prior to opening its doors for business, he returned to the states for three months. He arrived mid-morning, a package in his hands, and joyful light in his eyes. The warmth of the bright sun on a cloudless day invited outside enjoyment with a light jacket. I had prepared my small patio space for lunch the previous day, imagining the warming sun that showed itself.

My uncontained, pure joy as I greeted him grew the light in his eyes.

"Ah, such great joy to be present with all parts of your Beingness. I've enjoyed the communication shared through our souls but sharing our souls *and* this physical reality together is a rare gift."

He put his package down and helped to get lunch on my patio table. I talked of the beauty I felt coming to life through my musical performances at various symphonies around the country. "My experience with smaller symphonies is helping me to sense the unique, subtle nuances each orchestra infuses into their music, and to adjust my own music to it. No musical score I play sings the same song twice. Before bringing my flute to my mouth, I bring my breath to its hollow center where I connect with my spirit's light. In this silence, I touch the heart of the conductor while feeling the pulsing passions that flow through his or her blood and into the wand. When my heart meets the pulse of the wand, magic comes to life. My spirit's passion melds with the conductor's passion, and we become one pulse bound in passionate love. Its inspiration flows out from the wand's tip to touch and guide the hearts of the musicians. I feel sound lifting into the heights of passion's light, then descending into the depths of love's darkness. I couldn't be on this planet without the ceaseless growth of this magic within and without."

Antonio's eyes followed every word, the smile in them and on his face enlarging its presence. "You have blossomed into the magic of your spirit's sacred passion and your soul's sacred love. In ancient, mystical teachings, the wand symbolizes the force of spirit brought into manifestation as wind. It breathes life through our bodies from the second we are born, until the moment we take that final breath to exit our bodies. Our breath lives on as the pulsing light of our souls, and your breath is now integrating your soul's light within your transmuted human biology. From within the dark depths of your cellular void, spirit's life force is projected outward into the world through your breath of light. Both spirit and the sensuousness of life are extended, and that's why you find it almost impossible to be on Earth without your music."

"I've never felt disconnected from your soul after you left. Feeling your passion and love always lifted me while helping me to feel the presence of my own sacred Self. I often find myself touching one of your carvings. About a year ago, I sensed each carving radiating an entire universe of energies and stopped reading their cards. My mind was ready to fully embrace the knowing that the carvings held the wisdom of my soul. Its wisdom breathes through me *as* Me. Increasingly, my mind is trusting this wisdom and cooperating with it."

"I knew the day would come for you to discover exactly what you did. I'm not surprised given the light I see flowing through you. Let me get the gift I made for your garden."

The package was wrapped in a colorful tweed fabric with braided rainbow-colored twine attached to each side that held the fabric in place. Inside was a cedar wood carving of Kokopelli whose facial features looked much like mine. Its hair, much longer than mine, was in five braids that spiraled outward from the tip of his forehead to the bottom of his head, ending just before the neckline. Kokopelli could be dressed in the tweed garment of his wrapping. His feet danced, and the foot that was down had a notch on its bottom to attach a slim, stainless-steel pole. His hands held a small, bronze flute. Kokopelli's flute always had the mouth opening at its top, but Antonio said he felt the mouth should be on its side, just like my flute. His arms were positioned to support his flute.

"It's magnificent. I like Kokopelli holding the flute to the side. It will enhance the movement of wind through it. I know exactly where I want to place it."

"The bronze has extra tin mixed in it to help create sound, although Kokopelli's magic can create music through any medium. As with his robe, you can remove the flute as needed."

Kokopelli in my hands, and digging tools in Antonio's hands, we walked into my garden. The arriving birds were busy at the feeders. My garden was simpler and far rawer than Iris' garden, filled with shrubs of various colors and sizes. Flowers that did well in shade and the Vermont climate were the jewels that gave my garden its luster. The natural simplicity of the carving with the added elegance of the small, bronze flute captured my garden's spirit. Kokopelli's colorful native dress would lighten my garden when the sun left for what seemed as a very long vacation. I had dragon wing pink begonias the hummingbirds swarmed about during the summer, and there was a bench nearby where I often sat.

"This is my favorite spot to sit. I sense the freedom of the hummingbirds as they fly in any direction, even upside down. The vibrations of their wings as they hover are the song of an orchestra, and their solitary nature assures me it's fine not to seek friendships and activities to do." We began to prepare the ground for Kokopelli as we talked.

"I see your need for space continues. Have you dated at all?"

"Yes, after a couple of years in this orchestra, I dated a cello player for about six months. While she's committed to excellence in her music, she has a large family and several friends she likes to visit often. She tended to get entangled in drama, and I knew the relationship wouldn't work. We remain friends and occasionally share a meal together. I need to meet someone who knows completeness within all facets of themselves as human, soul, and spirit, and that person has not yet arrived."

"I understand," Antonio said as we made our way to the house. He made coffee as I cleared the table. While enjoying the coffee, he asked if I am away often to practice with other symphonies.

"I only accept work where there's good quality internet to do the preliminary preparation. I spend about a week away every two months or so to play elsewhere. I play solos with my current orchestra, and they don't want to lose me. It's working for now, but in two years, things could be quite different. What's important is that I'm expanding more deeply into the passion of my spirit and am learning how to move its presence through my instruments with extended grace each day."

Antonio said things will most likely be changing as my music becomes increasingly known. "Your experience with the smaller symphonies is helping to prepare you for what lies ahead. I don't want to scare you about your future, but I will share the strong potential for your music to be recognized on an international level. You have much to look forward to. I've already visited with Micaela, and she said each time she listens to your music, it's more pure, more passionate. Few people are willing to take the path you've taken. It was your destiny, and you didn't shrug it off to take an easier path. Doing so would have compromised who you've come to know yourself to be as a multidimensional Being, and the music you now create through all facets of your Beingness."

"I love having Micaela present when I play. More than once, she's traveled a distance to hear me. We always have brunch together the day after the performance to share insights about my music. It's like she has an antenna that senses when I'm getting stuck because she always seems to show up with that magical solution to help me break through emerging barriers. I've also continued to visit Brother Tom as often as I can find time to do so. I bring him new music, and he gives me a blank canvas and paints.

"He's encouraged me to paint what I hear in my music. When I finally released concern about my limited technical abilities, I was amazed at what my paintings revealed. Sometimes, I paint forms of nature I sense in the music, and other times, I paint abstracts. But what strikes me most is the colors. As I listen to the music when my painting is done, I find myself lightening or darkening a color. When I later alter my musical score by lightening or darkening a tone, it always enhances it. I know Brother Tom wouldn't concede his guidance in my music, but I recognize it. In fact, his soul's presence is becoming a regular guiding force, whether I'm in his presence or not, just as my connection to your soul guides me. It's just a different type of guidance."

"Your creative spirit inspires us as much as our sacred Self inspires you. It's a shared radiance, free of any attachments. I'm going to see Ethan and Iris next week. Micaela said there's big changes in them, and the lives they're creating, but wouldn't spoil the surprise by sharing any details. I'd have to see for myself."

"I agree with Micaela on all fronts. I usually see them every other month, and they sometimes come when I have a solo performance. They're quite busy with their own endeavors as you will soon discover. We all know our greatest strength and inspiration are sourced from within, and none of us feel dependency on each other for support. But we always appreciate sharing our creations with each other when possible."

"I'm looking forward to seeing them. It'll be dark soon, and I have a distance to travel. I say goodbye only as my human self that needs this physical reality to share time together."

After he left, I went into my garden to sit with Kokopelli. A breeze had been stirring over the garden all day, singing through his flute as if singing a lullaby for its oncoming winter slumber. I sat for some time, enjoying the harmonized symphony between the songs of the few remaining birds and the bronze flute. As I removed Kokopelli's colorful native robe, his music dimmed its presence. He was beginning the retreat into his dark depths as winter approached. Kokopelli knew time was needed for his spirit's raw passion to be nurtured and shaped within his soul's inner depths, until brought forth in the spring as sacred creations of renewed life.

On Wednesday of Thanksgiving weekend, I was on my way to Westchester. I got a very early start to visit Brother Tom on the way. I had new music to share, and he had my canvas and paints ready. We continued to share tea when I arrived while listening to my new music. It had become a sacred ritual where any distractions I may have entered with, left me. As I drank my tea, I closed my eyes to taste the depths of its nectar. Kokopelli's form emerged, dancing joyfully with his small, bronze flute held to his side. "Antonio's spirit loves playing the trickster at times. For uncountable eons, I've played a wooden flute with the mouth on its top. Admittedly, the new form initially threw my confidence, until I remembered that I am a master musician, and the form of my craft is not my magic's source. Blowing my wind through the horizontal plane of my bronze flute is opening a deeper connection to Earth's changing vibrations. My magic has always been your magic to claim. Embrace magic, not limitation. Allow your flute to give Earth's sacredness a presence. As you paint, put your mind's remaining doubt into form, and infuse it with the transmuting power of sacred love."

I painted myself as the doubting Kokopelli with the ground he seeded initially barren. He had seeded fear's limitation, not love's abundance. Then I added life to the garden, painting the shrubs and flowers matured into the fullness of their colors. Finally, I added the vibrant colors of Kokopelli's tweed robe and rainbow twine. The doubting Kokopelli realized the secrets of manifesting great beauty on Earth through his magical, sacred center. When finished, I told Brother Tom who he was. There were a few visitors looking at his paintings, and a young couple came closer as I shared Kokopelli's meaning. I was taken by surprise when they asked what it cost.

"We have a daughter who's seven. She plays the flute exceptionally well for her age. We'd love to give her the painting for her upcoming birthday. We believe she'd enjoy getting to know Kokopelli, who may inspire her budding talents." I told them there was no fee, but they insisted on paying me. After they left, I insisted Brother Tom take the money.

"Very well," he said. "I'll put it aside for a better recorder to listen to your music with."

As I usually did, I stopped at the café in town for lunch. The oak-lined street vibrated with retreating life as the trees emptied their limbs of the life they had supported. They were dancing energy beings, singing the music of Earth's decaying life through their dance.

Continuing my drive to Westchester, I thought of all Antonio now knew about Iris and Ethan. Iris had shared the suggestion of a production with a new vision of gods and goddesses. Most dismissed the idea of any person or god existing as a multidimensional Being, and the suggestion was Dead on Arrival. So, for two years, Iris played the roles of characters and goddesses who knew only drama and conflict while also staying aware of herself as a witness to the drama she acted in. But as her own inner work expanded, she could no longer participate in assuming their personas, even while aware of herself as a witness to them, and she left.

One of the writers contacted her shortly afterward, telling her the idea inspired him, and he had already written some notes for a production. He knew of people in the city who were also willing to help. They believed funding could be gotten through various grants on the premise that the work extended what mythology offered to culture. When some money did start coming in, he left the theater group and was working full-time with Iris. Her past college major in English now served her well. More importantly, her growing strength and confidence enabled her to imagine and create without fear.

Ethan continued to spend much time practicing his violin, reaching deeply into the subtle depths he wished to create from. As with Iris, his inner work was expanding, enabling him to increasingly attune to the sacred sounds he heard in the music at my birth. It was a slow, gradual process, as layers of "dug in" karmic energies, accumulated from this lifetime and the biological ancestry inherited, resisted change. But like Iris and me, he was committed to facing whatever needed to be faced to feel and integrate the deep love of his soul.

While Ethan used his computer software at times, his music originated from within, not through software manipulation of sound. Increasingly, he was recording soundtracks from his violin as his tool to share his work.

Modern classical musicians performing as trios and quartets were starting to know of him and becoming clients. The descent into chaos to churn what needed to surface and be accepted was slowly yielding to a more sensuous sound of inspired beauty.

However, periods of chaos came and went for them as their minds continually adjusted to the new energies they were slowly allowing and integrating, and that inner chaos was why they continued their work with Micaela. They recently shared her story that dissolving charged, negative emotions were like peeling off layers of an onion. The outer, sweet layers, with a small bite, were so appreciated for what they offered that it was worth the tears shed to peel them from their core. The hardened core, with its bitter bite, was ignored and rejected. It was not worth any tears shed to use it. So, the onion's identity remained as it had always been.

But once you risked tasting the core's bitterness, and appreciated its special enhancement to flavor, it was transformed into a delicacy. No tears shed could keep you from it. With all parts of the onion tearfully peeled away, appreciated, and transmuted through love, what had once defined the onion was dissolved. Only empty space, full of new potentials, existed. You realized you could imagine an onion as anything you wanted it to be.

They were learning to appreciate their heaviest, most charged energies that were surfacing and embracing them as a delicacy. As their bitter energy was transmuted through love, they imagined who they would become. I reminded them that the deeper they dove into the dark waters of their inner sea where their most charged demons rested, the higher they could leap into the most potent light of their spirit's creative potentials. They assured me that no amount of inner turmoil could stop them from discovering the fullness of what existed beyond fear. Freeing themselves from their mind's forceful emotions, to deepen the love they could know, was worth every tear shed.

What exists at the bottom of the sea, the heights of the sky, and beyond both? You, as soul and spirit, too. It is the space of imagination, where your spirit's burning passion is unified with your soul's sublime love. These creative potentials await their time to be touched by your breath and brought forward into time to inspire others. For the adventure of it all, take the dare of your inner devil to transmute your demons through your soul's love. Then spread the wings of your lightened mind and body and fly into the fullness of your Beingness. Manifest creations of loving passion and bring forth children of hope on Earth.

ABOUT THE AUTHOR

BETSEY GROBECKER has had a life-long yearning to know a deeper truth to her existence that could not be found in the teachings of western science and Catholicism of her heritage. Leaving her cultural truths behind, Betsey explored Native American Shamanism, Peruvian Shamanism, Indian Vedanta, and New Energy Consciousness while working closely with spiritual masters of these traditions. Her passion is to share her insights of the perilous mythic journey within, where all is risked to follow the calling of the divine heart and realize true magic.